The Running Boy

Written by Tyler from Perth
Edited by Nick Wactor
Cover Image by Liam Shannon

Bitchy and JP,

Wishing you all the very best for a beautiful wedding in these Hawaiian islands, and for every day afterwards. Bitch, you brought me to Camp, so I can thank you for these Four-Winds inspired tales.

TFP

For the Royal Boys,
Session One and Session Two,
To whom I told these tales,
And for whom I write
them down to be told
again.

Contents

The Forest of Broken Rules

There was no doubt about it; Alex was a dreamer. Andy often caught him out, during camp presentations or in a rowboat in a rowing class, during sports matches when the ball rolled right by him, or whilst everyone else cleaned the boys' bathroom and he stood staring out the window. Any time there was an opportunity Alex drifted off into another world and lost all sense of what was going on around him.

Andy thought it was kind of funny. That vacant expression on Alex's pale face often annoyed the other campers as they worked around him on the field or skillfully propelled their rowboats across the water. It was a clear sunny day when the two of them were sitting by the lodge, and Andy saw that look on his face once again.

"Alex," he asked curiously. "Where do you *go*? When you daydream, I mean. It's like you're in a different world."

"Oh," said Alex coming back to reality. "Well..." He said. "Maybe I'll show you. Later."

Show me? Andy considered this.

He was curious to see what Alex could possibly show

him. The next day after lunch, Alex pulled Andy aside.

"Do you want to see?" He asked with a glint in his eye. "Really?"

"Yes," said Andy, "show me."

The two of them ran off along one of the forest trails, Alex leading the way with a bound in his step. They ran and ran, until Alex slowed to look for something. He found a small and almost unnoticeable trail breaking away from the main. It led deeper into the woods and further from camp than Andy had ever been. The two boys walked single file between the trees, and the trail itself seemed to disappear. They tripped over roots and bushes as they made their way deeper and deeper into the wood.

Andy began to notice how unusual this was, this neck of the woods was. Firstly, how quiet and untouched it seemed compared to anywhere he'd seen. He doubted many other people ever ventured deep enough to reach this corner of the forest.

He looked around at the interesting shapes the trees made with their trunks and branches, and they often seemed so strange that they made no sense. It was as if the trees had changed their mind about which way to grow. Some grew towards the sky. Others grew halfway towards the sky before curving and growing back to the ground, or horizontally to the left or right. Though the sun shone overhead, Andy noticed the shadows cast seemed not to follow any kind of logic; they all pointed in different directions. Some trees even had no shadows while others had several.

The leaves in the trees shifted and swayed though there was not a breath of wind. Everything was warped and unusual. Finally, Alex stopped walking. They had arrived. They were in the centre of a clearing and for the first time since entering the wood they could make out the sky between the tree canopies.

"What is this place...?" Asked Andy.

"I don't know," answered Alex, "but this place is really different."

He smiled.

Andy explored the tree trunks around him. Some had strange markings that people had etched into the trunks with stones. Some had random words or messages.

"Why?" Andy asked, not fully understanding why they had come.

"I don't know *why* it happens," said Alex, "but nowhere else can you do this..."

Andy turned around.

"Do what-?" he began to ask, but when he realized what he was seeing, he froze. Alex was floating several feet off the ground. He was quiet literally, unbelievably and inexplicably flying.

Andy's jaw dropped. He couldn't believe this was possible. Alex returned slowly to the ground.

"Now you try," he said.

"How?" Andy asked. His eyes were wide and his hands were trembling with disbelief.

"You just... Look up, and then you push away from the ground. You just go."

Andy tried this. Instantly the weight of his body was lifted and he began to float skyward.

"Woah," he called down as he rose steadily higher, "Alex, how do I STOP?!"

"Just like you're swimming," Alex answered calming. "Just swim down."

Andy was almost beyond the tree canopies when he got the hang of it.

For the longest time, the two boys soared among the tree branches, honing their skills and showing off to one another. They forgot all about camp and that they were supposed to be somewhere, and in fact they forgot about all else. The simply laughed and played and had fun. The sky was the limit.

Later that day Andy woke up from a nap, tucked into his bed in his tent with the bell ringing for the next classes. He hurried off and was barely late. No one asked where he had been. It was strange — when he thought back, he didn't remember leaving the forest; he didn't remember coming back to nap in the tent.

Andy met up with Alex later that evening to talk about what had happened.

"Things don't make sense there," Alex was saying happily. "I call it The Forest of Broken Rules. Time seems to last longer, and science kind of stops working. When I'm there I'm never really sure of things, I just kind of get lost, like I do in my imagination."

Andy and Alex agreed to go back again the next afternoon. When it came time they were filled with wonderment. They trooped excitedly through the forest, noticing all the oddities as they went — the curiously shaped trees, the way the branches seemed to move with a breeze that wasn't there.

Andy noticed the markings on the trees as they approached the clearing.

He supposed they must be the markings of others who had found this incredible place.

The words on the trees were all jumbled up so that none of the messages could be read, but the words used were very interesting. Some would say "happy", and "free". Some said odd things like "Pumpernickel" or "Glass Globe Gobble-de-go". Andy found one that said "run away" and underneath it said "hide", "help me" and "poop". Alex was right – nothing made sense here.

When they reached the clearing again, the boys lifted into the air. They drifted about and let their imaginations run wild. It felt like hours they were there, with the sun shining endlessly overhead. They never got hungry or thirsty, they never got tired or bored, they simply played and played...

Andy woke again to the sound of the bell ringing for his next class. He ran off to his next camp activity, but really, his mind was on the forest. His friends caught him day-dreaming during a game of soccer – he had cost them the goal. Andy resolved to pay closer attention. He saw Alex later that day, sitting under a tree and day-dreaming as he hummed along with the birds. He looked quite pale in the summer light. But then, he always did.

The two boys returned again and again to the forest. They wanted to spend more time there than anywhere else at camp. There was nothing like that feeling of soaring so high above the ground, so high over their problems and worries.

One day Andy's counselor warned him about day-dreaming. He hadn't realized it had become such a big problem.

"It's almost like you're not even here. You spend more time in your head than at camp."

Andy saw that The Forest of Broken Rules had become more and more important to him, and resolved to spend less time there.

But when the opportunities came for him and Alex

to go, he couldn't resist. It was a place he could really be happy. And so he continued to go back again and again.

During the rest of camp he struggled to stay focused. His mind kept drifting off to better places. And then there was Alex. If Andy was bad at focusing, he was nothing compared to Alex. He sat paler than ever, day after day, class after class, just day-dreaming. He often looked so white, Andy wondered if he was getting sick.

They were on the way back to the forest one day when Andy told Alex about his worries. He told him that maybe they really should spend less time in the forest.

"Why?" Asked Alex. "We're happy there. Isn't that the most important thing?"

Andy didn't know what to say to this. When he got to the clearing and lifted once more into the air, he forgot about his worries. He forgot all about everything else was once again lost in the wonder of The Forest of Broken Rules.

When Andy arrived at his other classes later that day, he noticed that Alex was not there. He seemed to be nowhere, and no one knew where he was. For the first time, Andy became seriously worried. The next morning when there was still no sign of Alex, Andy returned to the forest to look for him.

There he was, soaring through the trees, happy as anyone. He had simply never left.

Alex came down.

Andy felt angry. He asked Alex where he had been all this time, but Alex told him to calm down, that everything was fine, that he was just having fun. But Andy noticed something about him. He really was sickly pale. But more than that, he noticed something very wrong. Not only was Alex pale, but when Andy looked at him, he could see the trees on the other side of his body. Alex had become slightly transparent.

It was as if Alex was fading away.

Andy demanded that they leave the forest right away. That they go back to camp, that someone by now must be looking for them. But Alex refused to leave. He took off into the air, and Andy followed him, trying to catch him. Alex laughed, and with his fine flying skills he managed to evade Andy's outreached arms.

Alex's voice echoed through the trees and Andy was unable to find him. He searched and he searched and he searched for hours, it seemed, and then eventually... He woke up safe in his bed with the bell ringing for his next class. Again, Alex was in none of his classes.

Andy, of course, knew where he was.

Andy was going back. He was going to bring Alex out of the forest, whatever he had to do.

When he got to the clearing he found Alex wandering aimlessly yet happily though the trees, staring at the odd shapes with a vacant kind of smile. He had no worries in the world.

"Alex," Andy called.

Alex turned to look at him.

Alex stared at Andy with an odd look on his face.

Andy's heart sank.

Alex had forgotten who he was.

And he really was transparent now. Andy was panic-stricken. Alex was slowly but surely disappearing. Suddenly Alex's face split into a grin.

"Andy," he said, "welcome back! Let's go exploring, shall we?"

"No, Alex, it's time to go now. Time to get back to camp."

"No, let's stay for a bit!" He said, with that silly grin. "Come on!"

Alex turned and ran between the trunks. Andy called out to him but he would not come back. Andy heard his voice. He was just out of sight. Alex was laughing and calling playfully back to him like some ghostly disembodied voice. Strangely enough, Andy heard more than Alex's voice. There were more people in this forest, more voices just out of sight. People laughing and giggling and talking amongst themselves, hiding between the trees.

Andy tried to follow the voices. He ran between the trees, and the markings upon them stood out to him, cryptic as ever. Except for one, that made perfect sense. This one, more than the others, stood out. It was a simple message, a clear message: a message of warning. Andy stopped to read it.

Come and play, your spirit aloft,
But come and stay, and be forever lost...

Andy tried to stay calm. He called out desperately to Alex, calling him back, warning him, pleading him to return.

All he ever got back was a distant voice, the sound of Alex laughing and playing, asking Andy to join him in the fun.

Andy woke in his bed feeling sick.

He didn't know what to do. He decided it was time to go and tell a counselor everything. After class he pulled one aside, telling him everything about what had happened, about where Alex was now, how he didn't want to come back. The counselor stopped him.

"Wait, who is in the forest?" The counselor asked.

"Alex, he loves it in there, he won't come back-"

"Alex who?" Asked the Counselor.

"Alex-" but Andy stopped speaking when he realized what had happened. For too long no one had been asking after Alex, and no one had come looking for him. No one had mentioned his absence or talked about him in conversation. No one had even noticed that he was gone. Andy asked others around the camp. Everyone he spoke to had forgotten who Alex was, had said there was no Alex at camp at all. Some people asked Andy if he was feeling sick, they told him that he should lie down. After all, he did look very pale.

Andy was in shock. He didn't know what to do.

He decided to return one more time to the forest, but vowing this would be his very last time. Later that day, as he walked between the oddly shaped boughs, he called out to Alex. The place was quiet and still as always. It was a lost place, The Forest of Broken Rules. It was a place for dreamers, a place where you go in your mind to feel better, to feel free. It truly was a dangerous place to become lost.

Andy searched and he searched, but the most he found was the sound of those carefree voices of lost people talking and laughing just out of sight. If Andy listened close enough, he could almost hear Alex's laughing voice among them.

The Praying Girl

There was a boy who came to camp, a boy who had never come before. His family and friends had told him of the many legends of camp; stories of scary things that had happened in the forests or out on the grounds, of things that were hidden among the trees and in the swamps and beaches. They told him all about The Clay Army, and of The Forest of Broken Rules. They also told him the story of The Praying Girl.

The story goes that somewhere in the forests of summer camp there was a tree stump that looked like a girl. Its odd shape and various growths made it appear that she was kneeling down to pray, her little face looking upward, her hands clasped tightly together. It was said that if you found The Praying Girl, and if you talked to her long enough, she just might come to life.

Well the boy loved hearing the stories and the legends, and was excited to finally come to camp.

He was excited to explore for himself and see if any of these stories could possibly be true.

When he finally did come to camp, however, it was not quite what he had expected.

The other boys in his tent were cruel: they bullied him every day. From sunrise to sunset the boy was pushed around and laughed at, and though he valiantly tried, he was unable to make any friends.

He worked hard to impress the other boys, to show them that he wasn't afraid, that he was worth their time. When they mocked him, he tried to change the topic and start up a conversation with one of them. When they pushed him into the mud, he would get up, find a ball and offer to kick it around with them. When their counselor had group discussions with the tent, the boy was not afraid to share and contribute, not afraid to share what he thought and what was important to him. But nobody in the tent cared what he had to say.

No matter how hard he worked, the boys never respected him. The boy's counselor tried to reconcile the tent, but the other campers ignored the punishments handed to them and never accepted the boy as part of the group.

One day the counselor pulled the boy aside and told him that even though he would continue to try to make the tent work, that it was a good idea for the boy to try to make friends somewhere else as well. The counselor gave him some advice.

"You are very tolerant," the counselor said to him. "You continue to be warm and trusting and open and with them, despite the way they treat you. You must be careful. It's not a good thing if they won't do the same in return."

The boy thought about this, but he really looked up to the other boys.

After all, they were some of the coolest guys in camp. He really believed they would come around. And so he continued trying to convince them that he was worth it. The harder he tried, the harder they were on him. The boy began spending more and more time on his own, upset and unable to face other people around the camp. He took walks on his own, around the cabins and tents, along the beach and by the lake, to the barn and through the forest. He could walk for hours on his own, unwilling to go back to camp activities.

Whilst he was walking through the forest alone one afternoon, he saw her. There she was, plain as day; a tree stump that looked like a girl; a girl kneeling down to pray. He approached her. She looked young, perhaps his age. She was kneeling on the ground, her hands together in front of her body, and by the solemn look on her face, she was certainly praying.

The boy sat down next to her and stared at her. After a little while, daring to wonder if the stories could possibly be true, he began to talk to her. Once he started talking to her, he couldn't stop. He talked and he talked about everything. About the boys in his tent, about how he felt and how this was not what he thought camp would be like.

He talked about how he missed home and wished he hadn't come. He talked for more than an hour, maybe even more than two, he couldn't be sure.

He was crying as he sat in front of her when he heard a noise in the trees around him. It was the sound of the wind blowing through the forest, and the leaves rustling on their branches.

As the wind passed through their little clearing, the boy saw something that made his heart stop.

The girl blinked.

The boy could not believe his eyes.

The story was really true. She was now still once

again, but there was no mistaking it:

The girl was coming to life.

When the boy came back the next day he again sat by her and he began to talk to her solemn face. He talked and he talked and he talked for the longest time, sharing everything with the girl. He laughed, he cried, he shouted with joy and fear and anxiety. There was nothing he didn't share with her.

After some time, the boy heard it again. The sound of the wind passing through the trees, of the leaves rustling on the branches with some strange magic, and he watched her. Surely enough, her eyes moved, just the smallest bit. It was like she was trying to look at him.

The boy was ecstatic. Just maybe he could bring this girl to life, he thought to himself, and then he would finally have a friend at camp; someone who would trust and love him, someone who would be grateful for him.

And so the boy went back day after day, and for hours each day he talked and he talked and he talked, he shared everything about how he was being bullied and about how he wanted to make friends and be happy. And with each passing day, when the wind blew in the trees and the leaves rustled in their branches, the girl would come a little more to life.

He continued going back, and soon enough the girl's face gained expression and she could look at him.

She looked at him almost sadly, understanding him, wanting him to feel better. After some time she could smile at him and even move her wooden head to see him better.

One day he was sitting by her, crying. The other boys had humiliated him in front of the whole camp.

They had told everyone such personal and embarrassing things about him, things he now regretted trusting them enough to tell them. As he sat there, something happened that shocked him. There was a soft voice in his ear, and voice said:

"Be careful."

The boy looked up. He couldn't believe it. The girl was speaking to him.

"Be careful," she said sadly, looking down at him. "Not to trust others with your story, if they won't trust you with theirs."

The boy was overjoyed. The girl was becoming more and more real every day, and now she could even talk back to him. He whooped with joy and hugged her, and together they sat for many more hours, talking quietly together about the other boys in the tent and what he should do. He continued coming back each day, sometimes twice a day, and she gave him great advice. She consoled him about what was happening and told him that it wasn't his fault. She told him that he was a great kid and that she was glad to be able to help in any way she could.

Over coming days she became more and more life-like as they talked about his life. There was color in her skin, her body was beginning to move, and her hands were almost as free as his.

Soon, she would be able to stand up.

If it weren't for those roots holding her to the ground, she'd be able to leave this place.

The boy continued coming back every day, and he knew he was close.

One day she looked so normal, he thought that if he came back just once more, those roots would fall away and she would be free.

So he came back the next day, he showed up bright and early, happy to spend all the time with her that she needed in order to become free.

He spoke with her for hours until he heard that wonderful sound: the sound of the wind blowing through the trees and the leaves rustling with that strange magic. The roots fell away from her feet. She stood up. She was finally free.

The boy had never been so happy in his entire life. He whooped with excitement, he leaped into the air with a joyous cry. However, when he turned to look at the girl, she did not look happy at all. In fact, she began to cry. The boy was confused.

"What's wrong?" He asked, "Why are you crying?"

"I'm sorry," she said, between sobs. "I'm so sorry..."

"Why are you sorry?" The boy asked, baffled now. This was everything they had wanted. "Aren't you happy to be free?"

"Didn't I tell you?" She asked, and now the boy began to feel worried. "Didn't I warn you not to trust people with your story, if they are unwilling to trust you with theirs?"

The girl took a deep breath.

"You see, it's my curse. I can't be free unless I have someone else to take my place."

The boy gasped in horror at this final betrayal.

He turned from the girl, he ran from her as fast as his feet would carry him.

He weaved between the trees and over the roots and shrubs.

But as he ran he heard that familiar sound behind him; the sound of the wind blowing through the trees and the leaves rustling with some strange magic. When that wind finally caught up with him, the boy was turned into a tree stump that looked like a boy running.

And if you go into the forest today, you can find him yourself; you can find the tree stump that looks like a boy running. And if you talk to him long enough, he just might come to life.

The Keeper of the Weary Moss Light

Some years ago, under the warmth of a summer sun, two friends had embarked on a camping trip in the islands. By kayak they moved from place to place and island to island, charting the currents each night by firelight. It was several nights into their trip when something caught their eye. From across the water and over the licking flames and sizzle of their dinner, shone a quiet and curious glowing light.

They pulled out their charts and they traced the location. The beach belonged to a small island by the name of Weary Moss. The island was not well travelled, nor well mapped. Most people skipped over Weary Moss Island for its larger and more popular brothers. Rory and Linda sat by their fire and discussed their options, but couldn't draw their eyes from the distracting glow on the other side of the water. When the two got up the next morning, they packed their things for a short journey; they had decided to investigate the mystery of the shimmering shores of Weary Moss Island.

The waters were still and quiet as they approached, their kayak silently carving its way.

They noticed the impressive cliff faces that ran along

the face of the island, and the incredible way their voices echoed back to them so loudly and clearly when they spoke. It was so loud and clear, in fact, that there was no need to raise their voices. Their casual conversation echoed back from the cliff face as if a teasing duplicate couple hid amongst the rocks.

They pulled up on the shore and began their search for a place to set up camp. There was no sign of the light on the beach, nor of any human beings at all. It was quiet and still and simple like the island they'd just left. What struck them about the island, though, was its unusual shape. It was split in two by a gorge. The two made their way to the top of the cliff face looking out over this gorge, and they noticed again how their voices echoed across the emptiness of the ravine. Their voices came so cleanly and easily back to them. It was a strange thing for their ears to behold.

The two had an idea. One would camp on one side of the gorge, and the other would camp on the other side, seeing as communication across the ravine was simply not an issue, and adventure was the name of the game. So Linda went down the side of the island with all her things, and then back up to the other side of the gorge where she found a place to camp. When both Linda and Rory stood opposite each other, and each could just make out the outline of the other across the empty space, they called out.

The sound travelled easily. They could have entire conversations as if they were speaking on the telephone.

The two set up camp separately and yet discussed their plans as they did so. Rory soon announced he would go exploring. So, he set off along the trails around Weary Moss Island, weaving through the forests and along the cliff faces. He noticed, as he walked, quaint little signs here and there about the place, advising him on what to do and what not to do on this mysterious Weary Moss Island.

"Rocky path ahead – wear solid shoes," one sign said.

"Keep our forests beautiful; please don't litter," said another.

Each one was signed the same way:

"Thank you very much – The Keeper of The Weary Moss Light."

When the path split in two he noticed one that made him chuckle. It said; "don't take this path, this one's boring. Honestly, the other one is much nicer. It has views. Thank you very much – The Keeper of the Weary Moss Light."

He chuckled and continued on as the sign recommended. As the sun had set, Rory was walking along a cliff face looking out over the beach and other islands. He was about to head back to his camp site when he saw something that made him stop altogether. Something that made the hairs on his arms stand up. As he looked down to the beach below, he saw a man. This struck him as strange firstly, as there had been no sign of him on the island since their arrival. The man, even stranger, was not standing still, but running, and running as fast as he could from the forest to the water's edge.

When he reached it, he paused momentarily.

He pulled from his pocket a small light, small but bright as a powerful lamp, and he tossed it carelessly into the shallows. He then continued splashing out into the water before diving head-first into the depths.

Rory watched, unnerved, as the man swam steadily out to sea, away from the island. Rory couldn't understand it. Where was he going now that it was dark, and did he really expect to be able to make it to another island safely? Why did he seem so desperate to get away without waiting for the morning light?

Rory made his way down to the water's edge to investigate and when he got there, the man was entirely gone. All that was left was that strange glowing light from the shallows of the water. He waded over to it and reached into the water. He pulled out a small stone that sat cold and hard in the palm of his hard. Perfectly ordinary it was, except for the fact that it glowed as bright as any flashlight.

As he stared at it, it dimmed calmly, content at his touch. He placed it in his pocket and made his way back to his camp site to rest.

That night, in the early hours of the morning, there was a disturbance. Rory woke abruptly from his sleep. He heard it clearly where he lay, and his blood ran cold under his skin. It was the sound of Linda's screaming. Rory scrambled from his bed to the gorge cliff-face. There was no mistaking it. Linda's screams echoed loud and clear to him where he stood.

"Rory, Rory help me, please hurry Rory! I'm falling, I'm falling Rory, help me up!"

He called out to her to hold on, and he tore off down the side of the island. He ran down to the beach and then back up the other side to Linda's campsite. By the time he got there, however, thecamp site was eerily silent. Rory feared the worst.

With blood rushing in his ears and his heart pumping in his chest, he peered over the edge of the gorge. It was far too dark to see anything at all. He began to call out to her as he panicked and searched her campsite. He stopped very quickly, however, once he peeked inside her tent.

There she was. Asleep, safe and sound in her tent, as if nothing had happened. He roused her, shaking her lightly, and in a rough and panicked voice he asked her –

"Linda, what happened? Are you alright? How were you falling?!"

She awoke confused from a deep sleep and hushed him.

"Rory, everything is fine, I'm fine, what are you doing here?"

"I heard you," he began to say, "I heard you calling out to me, you were falling."

"I wasn't falling," she said, confused and unsettled by his panic. "I was right here, this entire time."

After a moment or two of her assuring him that nothing was wrong and that he was probably just dreaming, he left her tent and headed back to his own. He lay down to sleep on his side of the gorge and it took him a while to settle and drift off.

In the morning he headed back over to see Linda. After breakfast the two of them explored the natural wonder that was Weary Moss.

They followed the trails and explored the beauty of the island.

The two of them noticed more of the signs from The Keeper of the Weary Moss Light.

"Beware of falling branches. Wood is heavy and hurty." said one.

"Please take care of our natural flora and fauna; it's

our pride and joy." Said another.

Always, they were signed "Thank you very much – The Keeper of the Weary Moss Light."

The signs were often quirky and unusual. Rory and Linda found one that said "Roses are red, violets are blue, red, red, blue, blue, red, blue, I'll steal your shoes."

They laughed at the strangeness of it all. This Keeper, they discussed, was obviously a very strange man who must have lived on the island a little too long. They had never seen this man, though, if he really was here. They also had never seen a home or a hut where such a man would live.

They continued to discuss the strangeness of the island as the two of them walked along a cliff face by the sea, when part of the cliff face gave way underneath them. Linda, who was walking on the on the edge, fell as her footing crumbled. She grasped wildly at a tree branch and held tight to it to stop from falling into the ocean below. She began to scream, calling out to Rory:

"Rory, Rory help me, please hurry Rory! I'm falling, I'm falling Rory, help me up!"

Rory grasped her arm firmly and pulled her back onto the trail and to safety, where she lay and hugged him as she sobbed. She told him that she had been so afraid, and that she was so grateful that he had saved her life.

But Rory wasn't really thinking about what she was saying.

He was thinking about what he had heard the night before, echoing across the gorge. He remembered Linda, calling out in precisely the same way now as he remembered it then. The two got to their feet shakily and headed back to the fire grate to cook dinner.

During dinner, Rory and Linda had argued. Linda had carelessly discarded a cheese wrapper, and Rory had confronted her about it. They were guests on this beautiful island, he explained. They had a duty to respect and care for it. Linda said that it wouldn't matter after they were gone. This made Rory mad. He told her he wasn't ready to go yet anyway, that there was so much to discover on Weary Moss Island.

As Rory headed back to his own camp site after dinner, he began thinking about the island and how it really was one of the most beautiful and most interesting he had ever seen. About how glad he was to see the sunset from the cliff faces each night, and walk the trails with the interesting signs.

He headed off the sleep easily that night, though it didn't last long. Once again, in the early hours of the morning, Rory was awoken by the sound, again, of Linda screaming. He rushed out to hear her screams echoing across the gorge;

"Rory! Rory, help me please! I'm drowning Rory, I'm drowning! Please hurry!"

Even as he heard her scream, he heard the sound of her gurgling as water filled her mouth and lungs. Rory ran as fast as he could, down the hill, down to the beach and up the other side of the gorge.

When he finally got to her camp site, he was entirely out of breath.

Once again, there was nothing but silence.

He hurried into her tent, and there she was, asleep, safe and sound. He roused her again, struggling to keep his calm.

"Linda, Linda, are you alright? Did anything happen to you just now?"

She awoke and hushed him again.

"Everything is fine Rory, I'm fine. You must have had another bad dream. I've been here all along."

But Rory was not willing to believe it this time, as he headed back along the long trails to his campsite. There was something about this place; this strange, beautiful, unusual place. He was filled with an inexplicable feeling as he lay down to sleep. A feeling that this place had much more to it than either of them yet understood.

When he woke up in the morning, the first thing he did was go to Linda's campsite to spend the morning with her. They went exploring together again, seeking out and sometimes laughing at the unusual signs left by The Keeper of the Weary Moss Light.

"Don't go this way," said one of the signs. "Too many brambles and I once saw a scary spider. Thank you very much – The Keeper of the Weary Moss Light."

Sometimes the signs were mysterious, and sometimes they gave advice.

"Mr. Snuffle-bum requests your presence at the top of baffle-bat rock. Two O'clock, Tuesday, if you please," said one.

"One foot, two foot, careful where you go in life..." said another.

Sometimes, Linda and Rory noticed, the signs were even rude or aggressive.

"If you break my branches, I'll break you," said one that was attached to a tree.

"We don't like visitors here. Watch yourself," said one in a clearing.

Always, no matter what, they were signed "thank you very much – The Keeper of the Weary Moss Light."

By this point, however, Linda was no longer finding the signs funny.

Rory tried to explain that they were supposed to be funny and informative. He suggested that maybe she wasn't taking the advice the signs offered, and that she should. After all, he said to her, she hasn't been treating the island as well as she should have.

Linda and Rory argued. Linda told Rory that he was being unfair to her, and that maybe it was time they left the island. Rory told her than he wasn't ready yet, that the island still had so much left to discover, and that she was being unreasonable. Linda and Rory took separate paths to take a breather from another. Rory was frustrated. He had seen her earlier that morning, tramping through the forest crushing shrubs and bushes carelessly. This was the most beautiful place. It deserved their care and respect.

Rory saw another sign that made him laugh.

"Oh Snufflekins, Snufflekins, where do you hide? You said that you loved me, but I know that you've lied! Thank you very much - The Keeper of the Weary Moss Light."

He began to follow the signs deeper into the forest. Some of them were very curious indeed.

There were two in particular.

They were the two that directly referred to something called 'The Weary Moss Light'.

Rory felt the cold stone that still sat in his pocket. It glowed so brightly at night.

One sign said "the only way to resign as Keeper of the Light, is to find another Keeper to take his place."

If this wasn't thought-provoking enough, another said; "he who finds The Weary Moss Light, becomes The Keeper of The Weary Moss Light." Rory lifted the small stone from his pocket. It glowed oddly in his hand. Could this possibly be it, he wondered? Could this be the Weary Moss Light?

As he continued through the forest, he discovered a clearing. Rory's jaw dropped. There were thousands upon thousands of Weary Moss signs. Stacked up on top of each other, lined up and leaned on trees, they were blank and stock piled ready for use.

Rory looked at the stone in his hand thought about all he had seen on the island. It did seem to make sense; the light glowing from the beach to attract new people to the island; The Keeper throwing the stone into the water before swimming away. It was crazy to think, but if he had the stone, then just maybe he had in fact become The Keeper. And if he was in fact The Keeper, then maybe he should act like The Keeper.

Rory picked up one of the sign and scribbled upon it with some discarded chalk.

"We take care of you, please take care of us. NO TRAMPLING. Thank you very much – The Keeper of the Weary Moss Light."

Rory took the sign back to Linda's camp site and planted it in the woods near her tent.

As he set it down, he heard a distant scream.

With the hairs on his neck standing on end, he knew exactly what was happening.

He set off, running as fast as he could towards the beach with the sound of Linda's cries getting louder and louder with each thumping step:

"Rory! Rory, help me please! I'm drowning Rory, I'm drowning! Please hurry!"

When he reached the ocean, he saw her stuck in a rip tide. He dived immediately into the water after her. She had never been a strong swimmer, but by swimming parallel to the beach, he managed to draw her back into the shore safely. She lay on the sand, sobbing, repeating that he had saved her life yet again.

The sound of her crying voice rang in his ears and he felt so thrown by this beautiful and mysterious island.

Could this really be happening?

Could this island be sending him clues and messages across the gorge?

Was this island able to tell the future?

Rory took Linda back to her campsite and made her dinner before the both of them lay down to sleep that night in their separate camps. Rory decided to sleep outside his tent by the gorge, just to be closer to that mysterious echoing void. Sure enough, in the early hours of the morning, he once again heard that sound of a screaming voice echoing across the island.

This time, however, was different. He lay still and frozen in his sleeping bag, paralyzed with shock.

What he was hearing from across the gorge he would never had expected in a thousand years.

Terror tore through his body, for not only did he hear Linda's screaming voice, but he also heard his own.

Linda was screaming, "No Rory, don't do this Rory, put the gun down Rory –"

And his own voice, calm, and purposeful, spoke to her.

"I'm so sorry Linda, but I have to do this Linda, it's for the good of the island, Linda..."

And following Linda's scream was the sound of a single gunshot, firing into the night, and then silence.

Rory did not get up.

He didn't move at all.

Yes, Linda and he argued from time to time, but he would never, in a million years, harm her. Rory couldn't sleep for the rest of the night, and when he awoke, he was so exhausted he couldn't think straight.

He moved to Linda's campsite early and made breakfast for her. They went exploring again together as the sun rose over the water. She was talking about when they would finally leave the island. This annoyed Rory, who wanted to stay longer, but he kept calm and let it go. The two of them did not argue, and when the sun began to set that evening, the two had enjoyed a great day together.

Linda was preparing dinner by the fire and the two were chatting pleasantly with a view of the beach and the other islands. Rory's tension had almost left him when suddenly he saw something.

Linda fell silent, watching him curiously. Rory was stony-faced and unreadable.

He got up and left the campsite. Linda, confused, waited for him to return.

Linda had noticed Rory becoming more and more temperamental since arriving on the island. She was aware of his mood swings and strange attitude toward the island.

When she saw Rory approaching with the gun, she stood up and backed away from him, screaming at him.

"No Rory, don't do this Rory, put the gun down Rory —"

"I'm so sorry Linda, but I have to do this Linda, it's for the good of the island, Linda..."

While Rory tried to explain, she got up and ran from

the camp fire, deep into the woods, away from the campsite and away from him.

Rory marched over to the cliff face over the ocean and stared down over the water. There they were: two canoes paddling their way towards the island. Two canoes full of strangers. He was filled with rage. He was The Keeper now. This island was his. He aimed his gun and fired a single shot towards the canoes.

Well, he missed the shot and it's a curious thing that the people in the canoe didn't hear it, with sound travelling so easily as it does on this island. Perhaps the island only allows you to hear what it wants you to hear.

Rory, breathing deeply and calming down, watched the strangers in their canoes as they paddled steadily to the beach. While they did, Rory watched as the figure of Linda arrived at the next one and jumped into their kayak.

She began paddling away from the island, away from the canoe paddlers, leaving him alone on the island to wait for them.

Rory returned slowly to the fire and put it out with the splash of a bucket. He left Linda's campsite and returned to his own.

It was now dark, and soon enough he headed in to bed.

He was woken in the early hours of the morning that night, strangely enough, by the sound of screaming coming across the gorge.

He got out of bed and stood by the cliff face, looking out over the beautiful island he loved. He listened intently to the sound of screaming voices; the screaming voices of the people in the canoes. The people who were now trespassing on his island.

He listened to the sound of his own laughing voice, which echoed cleanly back to him with the sound of gunshots firing from his rifle. Rory listened closely and calmly, and when all felt silent again, he smiled to himself before turning in to sleep once more.

The Old Story of Point Rocky

On the coast, there was a summer camp that was notorious and unpopular. It was said that the director of this particular summer camp treated his campers and staff poorly, and that the activities were arduous and grueling. The director ran his camp like the military, and forced all to participate in his regime until he was satisfied. He said that it built character to push the limits. He said that it was good for a person to struggle.

The thing was that he pushed the boundaries so much that the camp became unsafe. He would put young campers on dangerous horses, send campers out sailing in a storm, he would have them work in the camp's fields to grow fruit and vegetables for many hours a day. It's said that some kids ran away. Others plainly refused to come back the next summer.

When any authorities would come to the camp, he made the place look wonderful.

When parents wrote in saying that their kids came home unhappy, he would write back saying that conditions at the camp were excellent.

He would say that their children were probably just

exaggerating, and that they lacked spirit or character.

When the kids first arrived at camp, the director gathered them all together and went through a long list of rules, many of them ridiculous. He had forbidden odd activities he didn't like, like inkle-weaving and hay rides. He even forbade anyone from going to a place called Point Rocky for no particular reason. The other kids said it was a simple rocky point overlooking the water on the edge of camp property. The camp director said was unsafe.

It was a surprise that anyone continued to send their kids to this camp, but there were always new families that hadn't heard the stories. As the years went on, the camp director became secluded, and stopped coming out of his quarters except for special occasions. He began putting other members of staff in charge, much to the relief of everyone at the camp. Whenever the camp director was not there, all were calm and happy.

As time went on, and people saw less and less of the director. People said he had become moody and secretive. Kids would rarely see him during the summer, and when they did, he was grumpy and lashed out.

Jack was understandably nervous to come to camp when he heard all of the stories. But he was brave, and he did as his parents asked. He came to camp willing to participate and make new friends.

At camp he dreaded seeing the director, but when the director was gone it was a different place. He had a great time sailing and playing sports and singing camp songs around the fire.

He really was beginning to make great friends and have fun.

During the middle of the night, just a week after he had arrived, Jack got up to go to the bathroom. He wandered the trails in the moonlight trying to find his way. He soon realized that everything looked different in the dark. Before he knew it, he was lost. He climbed to the top of the hill in hopes he could scope out where he was. There was a gap in the trees as he walked and he noticed something. He could clearly see Point Rocky, a series of rocks on the edge of the water with one rock larger than the others.

The thing that Jack noticed, though, was not the point. He noticed that there was a flashlight pointed over the water from the large rock, and it roved back and forth as if searching for something. Someone was down there, at the forbidden point, sitting on the rock and flashing a light out to the open water. Jack ignored this and continued searching. He eventually found the bathroom, and found his way back to the tent easily. By morning, he had forgotten about the light at Point Rocky.

Several days passed, and again during the night Jack woke to nature's call. Jack found himself at the top of the hill looking out over Point Rocky on his way to the bathroom.

To his surprise and his curiosity, the camper at Point Rocky had returned. He or she was sitting on the largest rock with a flashlight pointed out over the water.

As he watched, the light moved slowly over the surface, and again it seemed as if the person was searching for something.

Jack stood and watched for a while, he didn't know how long. When it became apparent that the person was not going to leave, Jack moved on.

The next day Jack thought about what he had seen. He decided that that night he would sneak out to see if this person would return yet again. Night fell and Jack set his watch alarm before going to sleep. During the dead of the night he quickly hushed the bleeping of his watch and waited to hear a stir from his fellow campers. When it didn't come, he dressed silently and headed out for Point Rocky. He wandered through the trails along the water's edge and eventually found his way to the point. There he was; a boy about his age, sitting silently and alone on Point Rocky, looking out over the water with his flashlight lit, the circle of light moving slowly over the water's surface.

As he approached, Jack's foot landed upon a twig, and by the cracking under his foot the boy turned. When he saw that someone was there, the boy got to his feet and ran off into the woods before Jack do much more than call out to him.

Jack was left alone on the forbidden point, disappointed. He turned back and made his way slowly to his tent.

The next day Jack again decided to return to the point to confront the boy.

He was so curious about him, about what he was doing there and why he returned each night. He thought about the boy throughout the day and could not wait for night to fall.

When it eventually did, Jack set his watch alarm again and awoke in the dead of the night.

He made his way back to Point Rocky, and when he finally arrived, he was not surprised to see that the boy had returned. He was once again sitting on the largest rock, his flash light pointed out to the water.

"What are you looking for?" asked Jack, into the

silence.

The boy jumped up, afraid.

"Wait," said Jack, knowing the boy would try to run. "Don't be afraid, I just want to talk to you!"

The boy turned and hurried off into the forest. When Jack chased him between the trees, the boy disappeared entirely. Disappointed and frustrated with himself, he stood in the forest straining his ears for a sound, any sound. When he heard nothing, he returned to bed resolving to come back again the next night.

The next day came and went, and the next night was still and clear. When he found the boy again sitting on Point Rocky, he moved silently up and sat right down next to him. The boy turned fearfully to look at Jack, but did not move.

"My name is Jack," said Jack with confidence. "What's yours?"

The boy hesitated, but spoke. "Brian," he murmured quietly.

"Hi Brian. It's a good night for looking at the stars, isn't it?"

The boy didn't say anything. Jack went on.

"I like Orion's Belt. It reminds me of stories my dad used to tell me..."

Jack told Brian all about his dad and the stories he was told as a kid, and Brian listened.

As the minutes rolled on it became easier, and Brian was visibly more comfortable.

Brian even began to talk about what he liked about the stars. The two boys spoke for hours and Jack decided not to ask him yet why he came out here every night. It was very late when Jack told Brian that he should be going back to bed, but he would like to come back tomorrow. Brian nodded that this would be okay.

When Jack returned twenty four hours later, there he was, waiting for him. And again the next night too, Brian was waiting. And so the two boys continued to meet at Point Rocky night after night, and they became friends. Jack was often exhausted during the day, but did not stop coming out during the night to meet up with Brian. Jack asked him all about himself, and about how many summers he had come to camp and what he liked most about it. Brian began to chat more openly, sharing how he felt about this place, about how it scared him.

One night Jack asked Brian if he would be coming back to camp next year. Brian shrugged his shoulders.

"I don't really want to come back," he said.

"Why?" asked Jack.

"I don't like it here. Something bad happened here a while ago, you know. Not many people know the story, but I do. I don't want to come here anymore. That's why I sit here during the night."

Jack asked him if the camp director had been mean to him, but Brian just shook his head; his lips were sealed tight. No matter how hard Jack pushed to get more information from him, Brian said nothing else about it. As the nights rolled on, Jack said something to Brian.

"Brian, is there some way I can help you find what you are looking for out there?"

Brian thought about this.

"Maybe..." He said slowly. "But we would have to go out onto the water."

The two talked about it, and though Brian would not say what he was looking for, the two agreed to come back the next night, to take a row boat from the dock, and search for whatever it was that kept Brian returning to the same point each and every night. They agreed to meet the next morning, just before sunrise, before anyone else was awake, and then they could look.

All the plans were set, and both boys arrived at the dock the next night, just before the sun rose. However, when Jack got into the rowboat, Brian became very afraid. He said he didn't want to go anymore, that it was too scary. Though he tried, there was nothing Jack could do to persuade Brian. Jack offered to go out alone if only Brian would tell him what to look for.

Brian thought about this.

"Jack," he said. "If you go out to Point Rocky just beyond where that buoy is, and dive into the water, you will find it."

Brian said no more about this.

Jack was frustrated, but agreed. He paddled away from the dock and Brian was soon lost from sight. As the sun peeked over the mountains and lit the water, Jack arrived at Point Rocky, just beyond where the buoy sat bobbing on the water. Jack pulled off his shirt and stared at the cold dark water. He took a breath and plunged deep beneath the surface.

The water was deep and cold, and Jack could not touch the bottom.

He opened his eyes under the water - the sunlight was now beginning to penetrate it, and he could see. He surfaced to take a breath and then burrowed himself again into the depths. He swam down toward the sandy basin floor to search. He noticed a dark shape lurking not too far from him. After taking another breath he dove again, searching for the mysterious dark mass lurking on the sand. On his fourth dive, he found it. It was the remains of an old sailing boat that had sunk some time ago. He investigated it closely, feeling the wood in his hands. Just before he left the wreckage for another breath of air, he saw something. It was something green and ghostly, poking out from under the debris. Something terrifying that made Jack wish he was warm and safe in his bed. Something that made him wish he had never come out onto the boat, something that made him wish he had never ventured out to Point Rocky in the first place.

It was an old, decaying human hand, only just visible from underneath the wreckage. Jack panicked. He swam back to the surface and gasped for breath.

He swam, with adrenalin pumping, to his row boat and paddled as fast as he could to the shore. When he arrived, Brian was nowhere to be seen. Jack knew what he must do. He raced directly to the camp office to call for help, and within an hour, police officers and the coastguard were investigating the waters around the camp.

In the days, weeks and months to come, many things happened at the camp.

It was a week later that the camp director was arrested. Some months later he was charged with negligence, and was imprisoned for allowing a camper to drown under dangerous conditions.

It came out that the director had attempted to hide the death, claiming the boy had long since run away from the camp. The parents of the boy were finally able to rest, content at least that justice had been served. In years to come the camp became a happier place to be, with the camp director now gone, and thrived with many new campers and wonderful safe activities.

As for Jack, he went back to Point Rocky that very night after his discovery. Although he waited at Point Rocky for hours, Brian was nowhere to be seen. In fact, Brian did not ever return to Point Rocky after that. When Jack asked his counselors where Brian was, he was told that there was no Brian at camp this summer.

Jack tried to explain. He described the boy at Point Rocky, the boy with a flashlight. It was then that one of the counselors turned to him to ask;

"Are you talking about the Old Story of Point Rocky? There is a story; a story of a ghost of a boy who died years ago sailing out in a storm, who sits at the point, night after night. A story of ghost who sits with his flashlight, looking out over the sea, searching for justice."

The Boy with the Blue Paint

Six people, two canoes, and one camping adventure. That's kind of how all these stories begin. But this particular story begins just before these six people decided to go camping together. It all began in a living room in an ordinary home in the city. Six friends all gathered together, and one, Brennan, was telling the tale. "For you see, there is an island," Brennan was telling them, "and on that island is a small town by the forest. And in the outskirts of that town, on the edge of the forest, lived a very peculiar family of three.

"They kept to themselves. They rarely ventured into the town or even outside their large property. The mother and father were raising a small boy. They were loving parents, as it seemed to the boy, but very unusual things were happening in this home.

"Every few weeks, whilst the boy played quietly with his blocks, there came the sound of a human being screaming from the next room. The voice was always different, sometimes male, sometimes female, sometimes young, sometimes old.

The screaming would go on for hours, and then suddenly stop.

The boy never understood what was happening, but the sound would upset him.

He would wail and cry until his mother came in to comfort him. In order to keep him calm, his mother used to give him all kinds of toys and gifts and candies for when the screaming began, and as the boy got older, he became used to the sound, and enjoyed being showered with gifts and toys and affection. Soon enough, he even began to look forward to the screaming, he waited for it, he wished for it. And when it came, he was happy.

"The boy got older, and one sunny afternoon when he was eight years old he was playing in his back garden when the sound of sirens screeched down his street, and several large vans pulled into the driveway. The boy turned and ran from the house, into the forest, with the sound of doors being knocked down and the ringing of gunshots in the air. The boy ran and ran and ran until he had no more breath, and he was so deep in the forest that he couldn't find his way out.

"So the legend goes that one day the boy found his way back to his home, and he searched the dilapidated old house for his long-gone parents. Nature had taken over the house. When the boy could not find his parents, he returned to the forest to live forever.

And that is when the inhabitants of the town began to hear the sound of screaming at night, screaming that came from the forest, and the townsfolk then feared to enter it."

That is how the six people, in that living room in the city, came to the conclusion that they were going on an adventure.

They were going to the island, and they were going

camping in the forest; they were going to investigate the screaming that haunted the townsfolk.

And so they set out. They ventured to the island by canoe and delved deep into the forest. For days and days they ventured deeper and deeper. One day they set up camp and lit a fire. When the sun set they made s'mores and told scary stories, easily laughing them off as the night wore on. Brennan told the best stories and naturally laughed the loudest. Brennan was always the life of the party.

"What's that, Brennan?" asked Angela, who was sitting next to him. She pointed at his leg.

"I don't know," shrugged Brennan, frowning. "I must have rubbed up against something."

And so they ignored the curious blue stroke of paint on his leg, of which there was no explanation, and eventually it came time for them to turn in to sleep. Little did they know that this was the last time they all laughed together as one young and carefree group of friends from the city.

It was during the night that they scrambled from their beds in a panic, and in the dark outside their tents that they huddled together. It was the sound of someone screaming from some corner forest that had woken them. Someone hurt or injured or trapped; someone that needed their help. The six of them ran into the forest, following the sound, calling out to offer help, calling out to find their way. But they never could find the person; the voice always drifted away from them.

Quite suddenly the screaming stopped, and they were left alone in the dark and the silence.

After the minutes floated by, they knew there was nothing left for them to do but return to their beds. They eventually fell back asleep, and when the sun rose they woke and began making a clumsy breakfast, waiting for Brennan to come back from the bathroom before they packed up to move on.

But Brennan did not return, and the five of them discussed who had been the last to see him. As it turned out, no one was sure Brennan had gone to the bathroom, as they had assumed. In fact, no one had seen him since their venture into the forest the night before. When they thought back, they weren't even sure if he made it back to the tent.

They were each feeling uncomfortable now, and they sat in silence. When Brennan didn't return, they considered making plans to get out of the forest to call for help. This didn't make sense however; it was several days trekking out of this place, and several more for a search party to have any hope of finding him. Their only hope was to camp another night, and spend the day searching for him.

They set out into the forest as a group and scoured the area, but there was no sign of him. In the afternoon they tried again, searching for hours on end, but there was still no sign. When the sun set, they made dinner and discussed their next plan of action. If Brennan had not returned by morning, they would have to go. They would have to venture back to send out a search party for him.

They all had an uneasy sleep, and it was during the dark and the cold that they were all woken again by the sound of screaming.

As a group, they argued. Should they venture into the forest again to offer help, or just stand by as the person suffered, to keep themselves safe?

Unable to ignore the pleas for help, they ventured into the forest again, and again they were unable to find anything more than that empty darkness that held that elusive shrieking. No matter how fast they ran nor how closely they listened, they could never reach anyone or anything more than the same old trees. They stopped to breathe, the sound of screaming still ringing in their ears. This is when Angela pointed her torch at Emily.

"Emily," she asked. "What is that on your arm?"

They all looked, and sure enough, it was a strange blue smudge. No one was sure whether it was ink or paint or powder, but it was difficult to clear from the skin.

"Stick close to us," Adam suggested to Emily, worried.

But alas, within ten minutes, Emily and Angela had somehow been separated from the group, and the two of them stood alone, panicking and calling out to their friends from the darkness. Emily stopped and stared at Angela's arm.

"Angela," she said. "Not you too."

And there on her arm was that curious blue marking in strange ink, splashed carelessly across her skin from some unknown brush.

Back at the group, they heard Emily's and Angela's screams, but they never saw them again. The next morning the group, now just three people, rose sore and sleepless.

They were on the verge of panic. There was something very wrong with this place.

Someone or something lived in these woods, and whatever it was, it was slowly picking them off.

Over breakfast they decided they had to move fast. They were to march from now until sunset without stopping, and hopefully make it out of the forest to find help.

And so they packed their things and headed off, but

the forest itself seemed to have turned its back on
them. By sundown, they were entirely lost. It was a
tense meal around the fire, and between the three
of them no body spoke until –

"John," said Lousia. "Don't do that."

John was checking himself for blue markings. Pulling
up his pants legs, taking off his shoes. John stopped,
looking nervous and unsettled. They prepared a
single tent and they all curled up together inside it.
They lay awake for hours. Suddenly, they heard
screaming. Louisa and John sat up and realized that
Adam was no longer in the tent with them. Instead,
they heard him screaming from close within the
forest. The two burst from their tent and ran for him.
He sounded so close, and yet they could not find
him. They ran for hours, until the screaming stopped,
and then they ran some more, until the sun began
to rise behind the trees.

They wouldn't go back for the tent even if they
knew where it was. With rising panic and adrenaline
pumping, they were not back-tracking. They were
getting out of this forest. As the day wore on, Louisa
and John stumbled through the brambles under the
summer sun. They were now hungry and thirsty, but
they were so desperate to be out of this place they
cared about little else.

When the sun eventually set, they didn't stop.

They continued forward in what they hoped was a
straight line, looking desperately for something,
anything; a town, a beach, a hut, anything.

But nothing came. At three in the morning they
stopped to rest under a tree, and sleep overcame
them.

Louisa woke to the sound of John's screams, and
looked up to see him being dragged through the

forest, his face splashed in blue paint, his foot in the grasp of a hooded figure. She leapt to her feet and chased them, but like magic, they seemed to absorb into one of these many tree trunks and were gone with John's screaming echoing in her ears.

Unlike the others, John's screaming seemed never to stop in Louisa's ears. The sun rose and John's voice was still in her head, and she wondered if she was going insane. She stumbled through the trees and then she saw something. Tied to a tree branch in front of her was a small blue ribbon. She felt it in between her fingers. Ahead of her was another ribbon, and another, leading her.

She warily followed the blue ribbons, and she sensed the presence of another person watching her as she did. Someone was following her. She stopped suddenly in front of a large rock. Sitting atop this rock sat a tin can. She lifted it from where it sat, plucked the lid and peeked within. She didn't know what to think.

She set the can back down with the lid on top and she continued to wander. But the ribbons disappeared, and again in her path she found the tin can. Her mind buzzed curiously.

What was this man trying to tell her?

She carried the can with her, and the ribbons reappeared leading her way.

As the sun began to set after hours of travel, and Louisa began to recognize her surroundings.

That was the log upon which they sat one day for lunch. This was the clearing they set up camp all those happier nights ago. She realized that she was almost there; she was almost at the beach and at safety.

She raised her head; she could even smell the sea

salt on the air. This man, whoever he was, was leading her back to her canoe and to safety.

Weary in the dark that night, she sunk down under a tree and there she rested, awaiting whatever fate may come to her whilst she slept alone that night. When the morning came, she rose again from under the tree, alive and safe and unmarked.

She set off following the blue ribbons until she arrived safely on the glorious beach, her canoe waiting faithfully for her and her lost friends. She thought about the hooded man a she climbed into her canoe, tin can in hand. The boy from the story, now a man, and a clever man. A cunning man, a planning man, who loved nothing more than to hear the sound of screaming to remind him of his old home.

The girl placed the tin can in front of her where she sat in the canoe, and she opened it up again to see that it was still full of blue paint. She understood now what the man wanted her to do, as she pushed away from the shore.

The girl would never have returned to this island, never in a million years, had it not been for one thing. If it hadn't been for those screams, continuing, unceasing in her head.

It was some terrible curse that she was forced to endure those screams echo in her ears forever.

Every hour of every day, the screaming continued in her mind, offering her no peace.

There was only one thing to do the cease the noise. One thing, as The Boy with the Blue Paint had now asked of her. It was her duty to bring more people to this island, to this forest.

To wander through the trees and wait for The Boy with the Blue Paint to find them. It was her duty to mark with blue paint the ones that would scream the loudest.

Then, and only then, would the screaming in her head cease.

Lake Ann

In the forest there is a lake, and that lake is named Lake Ann. Supposedly, there is something wrong with the waters of Lake Ann. No one knows why, but people who go to the lake get sick. Campers are told not to go near the water – its murky-brown color and soupy swamp-like thickness make it a poor swimming hole. There have been stories of campers going into the lake and never coming out. There is definitely something about Lake Ann. People often wonder what's in the lake. How did it get this way? And why are some people afraid to even visit?

There are legends. It's been told there's a fortune at the bottom. A rich old man sank it in there long ago to keep it safe, knowing that anyone that went into the water would get sick and even die. Cody didn't really believe the story, but he wanted to know for himself. He wasn't afraid.

If there was something at the bottom of that lake, Cody was going to find it.

His friend Ben tried to warn him against it.

He said it was a bad idea, that there was probably a reason that people were afraid to go to the lake, but Cody didn't care. He was going in, and he was going all the way to the bottom. Ben woke up in the middle of the night to the sound of Cody fussing about the tent.

He really is doing it! thought Ben. *He's sneaking out to go to Lake Ann!*

Ben got up, and in hushed whispers he pleaded with Cody not to go, that at the very least, he would get in trouble with the counselor. But there was nothing he could say to change Cody's mind. Cody disappeared behind the tent flap and Ben went sadly back to bed. When he woke up in the morning, Cody had not returned. His counselor asked where Cody was, and they all said they didn't know. Ben held his tongue and tried to look innocent.

By the time they sat down to breakfast, Cody still had not shown up, and their counselor made the call: There was a camper missing. All camp gathered down on the beach to count their campers. Everyone was there, except Cody. He really was gone.

There was a camp-wide search conducted. Everyone was nervous, but none more than Ben. His hands shook with anxiety, his voice quavered when he spoke. The day rolled on, and they found nothing. Ben plucked up to courage to ask if they had checked Lake Ann. His counselor gave him a strange look. He asked Ben if he knew anything. Ben said he knew nothing, and changed the subject.

In the afternoon, a call came in by radio.

They had found him.

He was alive, but very sick. They found him in the forest, south of Lake Ann, unconscious and covered in brown muck. He had been throwing up for hours.

They took him into the health house and sealed him off from everyone. An ambulance was called to take him away.

Ben couldn't resist. He had to get into the health house and ask what had happened. He snuck around the back of the health house and peeked inside one of the windows. There he was, laying in bed, and still totally filthy. It looked as though they had tried to clean him, but the brown goo from the lake wouldn't shift from his skin. It soaked the sheets and the bed with brown ooze, and even leaked onto the floor. Cody looked very pale and diminished. His skin was white as chalk beneath the muck.

Ben slipped open the window and climbed inside.

"Cody," he whispered. "Cody!"

Cody looked around.

"Ben..." he moaned.

He looked desperate, and barely conscious.

"Don't let this happen to me Ben..." Cody was mumbling. "Don't let me become this..."

"What's happening?" hurried Ben, "What was in the lake? How did you get like this?!"

"Don't..." He struggled to speak. "Don't touch the water, don't disturb it... Ben, don't ever disturb the water... There are things in there... Things that live in there..."

Ben heard a noise at the door. He rushed back to the window, leaving Cody behind slipping into unconsciousness again.

The ambulance came and took him away, men with gloves and face masks helped him into the van. But only an hour later, they heard a strange and mysterious report. Cody was missing again. He had somehow escaped from the ambulance, leaving nothing behind but a huge brown soupy mess.

Ben didn't know what to think. As he went back to his tent that day something caught his eye. He rubbed at his hand. There was the smallest brown mark on his skin, as if from dirt or mud, but no matter how he rubbed it, it would not come off.

He tried to ignore it over the coming hours and days, but soon enough he could ignore it no more. Whilst the search continued for Cody, Ben was distracted by the strange brown mark. It was getting larger and larger every day, and it made him feel sick. He often felt nauseous and tired, and he struggled to participate in camp activities.

Fate, however, favored Ben. A few short days later, with the mark growing larger and larger and Ben feeling sicker and sicker, he and the other members of his tent were in the bathroom. One camper had gotten his hands on a can of their counselor's shaving cream. They battled with it, soaking each other in it until they had created a mass of soapy, fluffy white shaving cream, and each of them were covered. Hastily, they tried to clear their mess before heading back to their tent to sleep.

As Ben made his way to classes the next day, he felt better than he had in days. In fact, even the mark on his hand and arm seemed to have gotten smaller...

He thought about this.

During rest hour (after they had been forced to clean the bathroom by their counselor) Ben began looking for more shaving cream. When the bathroom was empty of people, he found a can on top of the mirror.

He applied it generously to his hand. The feel of it soothed his skin, and over the next hour, he could see the mark visibly reducing in size.

As he lay down to sleep that night, he thought about Cody, still entirely missing. He remembered one of the last things he had said to him.

"Don't let this happen to me Ben..."

Ben had one terrifying thought of where he might have gone. Ben had heard the stories. That night, Ben waited until the others were asleep before getting up and getting dressed. Ben thought about Cody. When you're covered in muck and filth that cannot be removed... Where more fitting to go than back to Lake Ann?

It was Ben's turn for a midnight visit to the forbidden lake.

He crept between the trees around camp, careful not to be seen. He needn't have worried; the grounds were empty. He walked along the trails towards Lake Ann. It was so quiet, and the moon shone so bright overhead that he barely needed his flashlight.

When he finally reached the lake, he was afraid. It sat cold and still, and as filthy as ever. He pulled from his pockets two cans of shaving cream stolen from bathrooms around camp and held them tight. He approached the edge of the water.

Standing poised and ready, he placed his foot on a large log and kicked it into the water.

With an incredible SPLASH the log bobbed away on the surface of the water, and Ben waited.

It took ten seconds, and Ben heard the most incredible sound. The sound sent a shiver down his spine and his skin tingled with foreboding. It was an animal-like cry, shrill and cold, and most horrifying to the ears.

The water surface did not settle after the log had

disturbed it, but in fact it began to stir. On the other side of the lake, a human hand burst forth from the water, covered in muck and filth. Suddenly, everywhere Ben looked horrible swamp monsters were emerging from the water, crying out and screeching, their skin decomposing and their faces unrecognizable. Some were children, some were adults, but all of them stank like rotting garbage.

When Ben hit them with the shaving cream, they screeched and pulled back in burning pain. As they came for him, he hit each and every one of them. But he searched as he did, for one in particular he was looking for.

He emptied one can of shaving cream as he battled his way around the lake, the screeches of suffering monsters in the air. His second can was almost empty when he saw it. Dangling from the wrist of one of the horrific beasts, there was a very familiar friendship bracelet. In fact, it was the very same friendship bracelet that Ben had made for a very good friend of his, a friend by the name of Cody.

Ben remembered again what Cody had said to him, as he drained the last of his shaving cream on what remained of his good friend.

"Don't let this happen to me Ben... Don't let me become this..."

The creature that was once Cody screeched and cried, but surely enough he hit the ground and stopped moving. It was done. Ben had done what he had come here to do, to stop Cody from becoming the very thing that had claimed his life. But now, the creatures had him surrounded on all sides, and he was entirely out of ammunition.

When the sun rose in the morning, Ben's counselor noticed that yet another of his campers was missing.

When Ben did not show up to breakfast, his counselor called in another missing camper. The entire camp gathered on the beach. The entire camp, that is, except for Cody and Ben. A camp search was conducted, and Ben was not found anywhere on the grounds. It was then that the police called camp.

Reportedly, a shop keeper had come to work that morning to find that his store had been broken into. The odd thing was that the culprit was still inside the building. He had found a boy down the bathroom goods isle, asleep on the floor and covered from head to foot in shaving cream.

The Isle of the Inner Eye

There is an island on the charts and maps that remains unnamed even to this day. Entirely uninhabited, people on nearby islands rarely comment on it or have much to say about it. If you were to go asking, many would say they know nothing at all about it. Some, however, would have something interesting to say. Those who have lived in the islands long enough have heard noises coming from it. Inexplicable noises, different each time and never making sense. Some say they've heard loud and raucous parties on the island. Other say they have heard the sound of avalanches or earthquakes or of strange creatures and animals that they have never heard before.

One man claims that he once had a conversation with the island from his beach house porch facing out over the water. Another told the story of his brother, who died trying to swim to the island, after hearing someone calling out to him for help from its shores.

There was even an old woman who claimed that the island had been changing shape for years, and nobody had been documenting it well enough to know.

Those who have heard these noises often refer to the place as "The Isle of the Inner Eye", though no one is willing to explain what that means. Few people ever journeyed to the island. No ferry would take you there, and there was no dock for a boat. Occasionally, and very occasionally, someone would camp on the island. Apparently, people often never came back.

Too bad for Casey that she had not heard these stories. Casey was leading a kayaking trip, and it was during this kayaking trip that she decided to make a stop over to explore this unnamed land mass that she spied on her charts. She led the way, paddling strong for the shore, but as she did, a strange sound met their ears.

It was the sound of a hundred people chanting over and over again, one single word. The kayakers looked curiously at one another – they had believed this island to be uninhabited. But there it was, clear to their ears as the sound of their paddles entering the water: the sound of a group of people, hiding somewhere just out of sight, chanting this one word over and over again as they approached.

Fourteen.

Fourteen.

Fourteen.

Fourteen.

The chanting stopped as they pulled up on the shore. They began to set up their campsite, setting up tarps to sleep under and a fire to cook dinner.

Casey went looking for wood for the fire, and as she stomped through the forest she looked out for any sign of human life, of any signal that there might be others living or camping on the island, but there were none at all.

She wandered between the tree trunks stopping here and there to poke into bushes for wood. She stopped when she heard a low rumbling coming from beyond the rocks and growths in front of her. As she listened, the rumbling got louder and louder, and within a few moments it had become deafening. The ground itself vibrated and shook, the trees began to rock and shake where they stood. Casey very quickly came to her senses;

Something big was coming her way.

She turned back the way she came and began to run, dodging between the trees and finding her way back to the beach. She could hear the rumbling of a thousand heavy feet hitting the ground, and coming closer with every passing second. She knew she would not make it to the beach. She found a boulder and dove behind it, pulling her arms and legs into herself as she crouched under its protection.

All around her was a herd of every kind of animal; from Rhinos and elephants, from monkeys to giraffes, from sea otters to falcons, and everything in between. Animals from all around the globe had found their way to this island, and now Casey was stuck in a stampede.

Everything shook and the sound deafened her ears, but she sat still and low and waited. And sure enough, the sound began to pass, the stream of animals thinned, and she was left in the wake of the stampede.

When the last polar bear had made its way following the others, she got shakily to her feet. Drawing a deep, rattling breath, she calmed herself and headed back to the beach. When she got there, Rebecca was lighting kindling in a fire pit she had made from rocks.

"Did you hear that?!" Casey called excitedly as she emerged onto the sand from the wood. "Wasn't that the craziest thing in the world?!"

"Wasn't what the craziest thing in the world?" Rebecca asked, looking up at Casey, confused. "It's been quite peaceful here with you gone," she joked.

"You never heard that? At all?!"

Rebecca shook her head and Casey exhaled loudly, trying to think how to explain, knowing Rebecca would never believe her.

"A stampede!" She tried. "A massive stampede of every animal in the world – they all live here on this island! I almost died, I really did, they would have crushed me, but they passed me by..."

Rebecca's jaw dropped as she heard Casey's story. To think such animals could survive on this tiny island!

After dinner everyone went to bed and eventually fell asleep.

The next day, Casey and Rebecca went exploring. The day passed slowly by with trips up the hillside and to the beaches around the island. By the time the sun set, Rebecca had gone back to camp while Casey continued on. She was walking through the wood not far from camp when she saw a man standing up ahead. It was really getting dark now.

She crept slowly up to him, cautiously, suspicious.

Who could be hanging around the wood near their camp site? Who else was on this island anyway?

She had the impression that they were totally alone. When the man turned his head, she saw that it was only Michael – one of their fellow campers. She breathed a sigh of relief.

"Michael!" She called out to him. "What are you

doing?"

He turned to answer her, "just looking for Ed. Have you seen him?"

Michael and Edward were great friends, and had insisted they come on the trip with Casey and Rebecca. They promised to pull their own weight, and so their trip ended up with four people instead of two.

"I haven't seen Edward, come to think of it..." She said.

"What a strange island this is..." Michael said slowly, looking around. "Have you seen? I just came from a steaming orange mud bath I found in the forest. Orange, can you believe it!"

The two of them decided to explore together. Weaving between the trees, they made their way deeper and deeper into the forest. As they did, they were surprised to hear the sound of laughter. It sounded as if a man were laughing, chuckling to himself almost, just beyond the trees around them. They continued to walk and the laugher seemed to change locations. Once here, once there, then suddenly somewhere else.

Very suddenly, a face poked out from behind a tree. Casey and Michael were startled. It was the face of a middle aged man covered in clown makeup.

He laughed at them, withdrew his head, and disappeared entirely.

"Hey!" Casey called out. "Who are you?"

The man was gone, but she could still hear him laughing. She and Michael chased the sound of his voice until they reached a clearing. That was where the man leapt joyfully out at them. He bounded forward and stopped in front of them, dressed entirely in a clown suit; big floppy shoes and all.

"Hellloooo!" He laughed at them.

Casey and Michael were so taken aback that they didn't respond.

"I know what you're doing..." He said simply.

They stared at him.

"You want to dance the tango with a German the Arctic Circle!" He giggled and whisked himself off into the trees. His laughter died completely and Casey and Michael were left standing in silence in the field. They did not pursue him.

The two decided to head back to camp. There was definitely something strange about this place. On their way back to camp the two of them stuck close together and took care not to get lost. Casey began to smell something suspicious, but it was so faint on the wind she wasn't able to place what is was, until –

She stopped dead in her tracks. She sniffed at the air, and Michael looked at her curiously. Panic stricken, she listened closely to the silence and strained her eyes for any sign.

"Shhhhhh," she murmured when Michael tried to move.

She heard it. The crackling sound of a forest fire. She could smell the smoke on the air.

Looking up into the canopy of the trees, she could see the smoke spiraling into the sky from all around them.

"C'mon!" She yelled, panic stricken, and bolted back to camp with Michael. When she got there, Rebecca was gathering firewood to cook dinner.

"Rebecca!" She called, "Where is Ed, have you seen Ed?!"

"W-what?" She asked, uncertain.

"There's a fire, Bec, we have to..." But she trailed off.

From the beach she scanned the dim skies for any sign of smoke or fire.

There was nothing. Michael shrugged.

"Did you see the fire? It... Was huge, there was smoke!"

"No..." Rebecca spoke tentatively. "Perhaps... It was your imagination?"

The night rolled on and Edward showed up unharmed an hour later. He was gathering more fire wood. But Casey noticed that Rebecca seemed upset about something, or nervous, but she wouldn't say why.

They all turned in to sleep and during the night, something woke Casey from inside the tent. It was a curious sound, possibly the most strange and unexpected thing to hear in the wilderness. It was the sound of music. She stepped out of her tent to listen closer.

Yes! There it was! The sound of a fully-attended orchestra! She could hear the violins, the cellos, the trumpets, the French horns! She even thought she could hear the tinkling sound of the triangle from where she stood.

She followed the sound into the wood, searching for the source. As she wandered, the music grew louder and louder. As she followed it, she stumbled across someone. Much to her surprise it was —

"Edward! What are you-"

"Shhhh," he said. He pointed ahead of him.

Standing next to him, Casey followed his gaze between the tree trunks. Ahead, illuminated by the moon, was a clearing. They both approached and their jaws both dropped when they saw it.

It was a marble ballroom open to the streaming moonlight, complete with full orchestra and playing the most beautiful music they had ever heard.

In the centre of the dance floor there danced a man and woman, dressed in a cocktail dress and tuxedo. Edward and Casey watched and listened, and time drifted slowly by. They couldn't be sure how long the two of them stood there. Perhaps a minute, perhaps an hour, maybe many hours.

Eventually, they tore themselves away from the music and the dance floor.

"C'mon," said Casey, "We should go back."

But Edward was gone. Disappeared entirely. She made her way back alone, and as she did, the strangeness of this place continued to find her. It was the sound of a child's laughter meeting her ears. As she walked, she heard it again, and she searched for the boy. And suddenly, there he was. He was skipping through the trees, laughing and giggling and totally alone, though it was the middle of the night. She followed him, but he began to hide from her. When she found him, he would run off laughing, and try to hide again.

"Stop," Casey said. "This isn't a game. Where are you parents?"

But he ignored her. She continued to follow him, and she found him dragging a kite over tree branches. He looked so sad when it didn't fly.

"What are you doing?" She asked. "You shouldn't be playing in the middle of the night."

He stood there and stared at the floor.

"She does..." He said.

"Who?"

"That Rebecca girl... I saw her tonight."

Casey didn't know what to say to this. Rebecca was asleep in her bed, not going into the forest late at night.

"Casey!" called a voice.

Casey looked around. It was Edward and Michael. Out of the corner of her eye, she saw the boy run off into the trees.

"What are you both doing up?" She asked them.

"It's Rebecca," they said, "she's up and running through the forest. We saw her. She was crying."

Sure enough, when the three of them made their way back to camp, Rebecca was not asleep. In fact, she was crying hysterically, sitting by the dead fire place, and when they arrived, she jumped up and ran over to Casey to hug her.

"I-it w-was horrible..." She cried. "Blood, blood everywhere..."

Casey sat her down and told her to breathe deeply. When she had calmed down enough, she explained what she had seen. She was wandering through the forest to go to the bathroom when the trees and bushes around her had started to bleed.

Blood came from everywhere, from the ground, from the rocks, from the sky, flooding the forest floor. She had run back to camp for safety when they had come and found her.

When Casey lay down to sleep, she wondered about this place.

What was happening?

How was all of this possible?

What was this island?

And Casey wondered about Rebecca. This place was strange, but Rebecca was not adapting very well. She had been acting strangely since first coming to the island. Cold and distant, erratic... This worried Casey most of all. Could this island be getting to her?

When they all woke in the morning, everyone had calmed down. They all explored together, had fun together, ate and went swimming together.

Though Rebecca had calmed down, she began acting even more unusually as the day went on. She got quieter and quieter, and seemed quite anxious. It seemed almost secretive to Casey, the way she wouldn't talk about things. At one point she even snuck off into the forest, and wouldn't explain why.

When the four of them sat down to dinner, things had gotten quite tense. No one spoke. All of them were wondering the same thing.

What was wrong with Rebecca?

And was she going to go venturing into the forest again tonight, like last night?

Casey didn't quite believe that Rebecca had needed to go to the bathroom. According to Michael and Edward, she was very far into the forest and acting very strangely. Casey decided that if Rebecca got up in the middle of the night, she would follow her.

During the middle of the night, Casey heard Rebecca get up from her sleeping bag, dress quietly, and head out into the night. Casey, as quietly as she could, followed her. Casey hung far back to not be heard.

Rebecca wandered on and on, and as she did, she seemed to become upset.

"GO AWAY" She yelled at a tree. "No, no, no! This can't be! Keep me safe!" she asked of a squirrel.

Casey watched her, afraid. Rebecca stopped and stared at a tree for about sixty seconds. Suddenly, she screamed, a high-pitched, terrifying, shrill scream. She bolted off between the trees, and Casey was left with her heart beating and adrenalin rushing through her veins.

Soon after this, Casey began the walk back to the campsite. As she did, however, a voice called out to her. It was Edward and Michael.

"There's definitely something wrong with Rebecca," Michael said. "I think she's really losing it."

Edward agreed. The three of them talked about it. Casey was so worried for her. They decided that in the morning, they would leave the island and try to get Rebecca some help. As they spoke, they heard someone gasp from behind them. It was Rebecca. She was eavesdropping on their conversation. She turned and ran off into the trees before they could confront her.

When they got back to camp Rebecca was not there. When the sun rose in the morning, she was still gone. In fact, she never came back to camp, even as the day wore slowly on. Now Casey was very worried. She discussed this with the other two. They would have to go into the forest and find her.

They would have to bring her out, by force if they had to.

And so, their search began. All day they searched, and found nothing. Even as the sun set, the three had a small meal and headed back into the forest to find her. They needed to get her back to the mainland before she hurt herself or anyone else.

As the night wore on, they were walking and walking when suddenly there was a dull thud on a tree trunk near Casey's head.

It was an arrow. They were under attack. They divided up and ran for their lives, scattering into the forest. When they finally met up, they were gasping for breath.

"It... Was... Rebecca..." Gasped Edward. "She's found a bow and arrow. She's trying to attack us!"

The three of them couldn't believe it that she would actually try to hurt them! She really was dangerous.

They had to stop her at any cost.

They searched the whole night through, and even split up to triple the search. Well, eventually, it was Casey that found her. Rebecca looked rabid and wild as she stood by the cliff face, staring at the moon over the water. She had a terrified look about her, and it was clear that the island had affected her. Casey confronted her, trying to reason with her, but there was no reasoning possible. Rebecca really had lost her mind.

Rebecca lashed out in anger, pushing Casey who fell backwards into a tree. The tree shattered as if it was made of glass, and Casey pushed her back. The two of them tussled and fought, stumbling into trees and bushes and rocks that each shattered beneath them like delicate hollow glass ornaments.

Soon the floor was a mess of sharp and shattered glass shards that cut into the both of them, and new glass trees seemed to sprout where the old ones had stood.

Casey didn't mean to do it. It was in self-defense she had tried to throw Rebecca off her. But Rebecca had tripped over a tree root, and before Casey knew it, she was tumbling over the edge of the cliff and into the sea.

Casey was in shock. Her hands shook and her breath rattled.

She headed back to camp, not knowing what she would say to Edward and Michael. The sun was rising by now, and the two boys were nowhere to be found. She began packing up the camp site.

They were leaving today; there was no sense in staying. When the camp was packed up, she took everything down to the water's edge where their kayaks sat waiting. Except there was only one kayak for some reason.

There should be two, each seating two people. Perhaps, Casey thought to herself, Edward and Michael were using theirs to look for Rebecca by skirting the island. Two hours passed, and when the boys did not come back, she decided she was going to leave without them. She climbed into her kayak and pushed away from the shore. As she paddled, she noticed something that made her think.

This really was a strange place. After all the things that had happened, it was difficult to tell the difference between what was real and what was in your mind.

She looked at her kayak. In the empty seat in front of her sat one of two water-proof food boxes. Casey remembered packing the boxes with Rebecca.

How they had laughed as they worked, christening each food box with a name, as if they were real people journeying with them.

What a strange thing...

She felt uneasy now. She thought back to last night, back to some of the last things Rebecca ever said to her.

"You're mad!" She had shouted. "You're seeing things! Imagining people! There is no Michael! There is no Edward! You're imagining everything!"

Casey felt confused as she sat in her kayak paddling away from the shore. She looked at the name christened on the first food box.

"Michael" it said, glistening in the morning sun. She looked back at the second food box pushed down between her feet.

"Edward" it said, plain as day.

Casey felt sick with confusion. It was a strange thing, as she paddled, but that chorus of chanting started up again.

The same chanting from the day they first arrived. One word, over and over again, but this time, it was a different word. It was no longer "fourteen, fourteen, fourteen, fourteen."

Casey shivered in a cold and uneasy way.

"Fifteen," came the chanting.

Fifteen.

Fifteen.

Fifteen.

Fifteen...

The Rumbling

In a tent on a summer camp's boy's side, five boys and their counselor lay sleeping. Only five lay sleeping; the sixth one lay awake, wide awake, for the sound of rumbling kept him uneasy.

They had all heard it. At night when they all lay down to sleep. It was a strange rumbling that would resonate over the grounds, low and quiet. No one could tell where it came from. It could easily come from the forests, so large and open that anything could be in there. The sound moved easily over the smooth surface of the sound waters, making the boy wonder if it came from one of the other islands or from the other side of the bay. It could come from the old abandoned house they're seen on the grounds, or from the camp director's house — he always seemed so strange, after all. Wherever it came from, no one could tell what made it, or could possibly imagine what could produce such a sound.

The new campers each year often talked about it, though they were quietly forbidden by the staff. The old campers had 'gotten over it', so they said. Bored by it, apparently.

To them, the stories and rumors had grown old.

They had learned to ignore it through the night. Whenever someone brought up the topic with staff or senior campers, they were quickly shushed and the issue was simply never addressed. Whenever the question was raised amongst those with a looser tongue, the tales were discussed in hushed voices of people disappearing all over the island.

There was a story that a reporter once came here to find the truth, living in the nearby town. No one would tell him a thing. He was struck by the strange, quiet nature of the island's inhabitants and so he kicked up a fuss all about the town. He tried to provoke them into saying anything at all about the mysterious rumbling, but no one ever did. One day he simply disappeared, and nothing of his research was ever published.

It was one of those things that no one would ever be able to explain, because the only ones who knew the truth were no longer around to tell about it.

The campers were on a tight schedule each day. All day they played and learned and worked on projects, but when dark came, they were ushered into their tents, no matter what. On the first day of camp the heads informed them that they must, under no circumstances, leave their tent after night fall. It was dangerous in the darkened hours, they said, even with a flashlight one could trip or get lost.

And so, without fail, they all filed into their tents each night as the sun set and as they crept into bed, that ominous sound of rumbling would ease itself over the quiet grounds. They slowly learned to ignore it, and for many of them, it lulled them to sleep.

But not Adam. It kept him awake. It kept him curious.

No one he spoke to knew anything about it. It drove him nuts to lie there each night not knowing the answer to question everyone else had given up asking. As Adam lay there, he made a plan. He was going to find out what was going on. He was going into the forest.

The next day he scoped out the camp's grounds. He explored the swamp and the beaches; he trooped off around the forest boundary by foot looking for trails and paths while the others were cleaning up after lunch. When night fell, they were all once again inside their tents. Their counselor was telling them a story about an oddly shaped tree stump in the forest. As they lay in their beds, staring blankly at the bunk above them or at the canvas ceiling with that same rumbling so strangely lingering in the background, the boys slowly drifted to sleep. When the story ended, their counselor lay down in his bunk, curling up under his sheets. Shortly thereafter, his slow breathing told Adam that he had fallen asleep. Adam lay for a while, and when he was sure it was safe, he slipped from his bed and dressed.

He stepped out of the tent and stood in the dark. He could hear it, distant but steady.

It must be mechanical.

Adam listened as closely as he could.

Or could some animal or group of animals make that sound?

He began walking between the other tents, following the sound. He followed it away from boy's side. He stood by the edge of the forest now.

He stepped onto one of the forest trails and continued to follow the sound. It slowly but steadily grew louder in his ears; he was going in the right direction. He came to something of a fork.

The trail naturally curved one way, but the sound was coming from another. Adam left the trail and strode fearlessly into the darkened wood.

Adam was walking ten minutes before he came across a sign. It was old, it was rusted and overgrown. It was printed with two sentences.

Keep the silence.
Keep the peace.

Adam didn't know what to make of this. He continued on, trying to follow the sound, his ears straining to listen. The further he went into the forest, however, the less he was able to follow the sound of the rumbling. At one point it was coming from his left; then it seemed to be coming from his right. For one frightening moment, it seemed to be coming from behind him. Increasingly, it seemed to be coming from everywhere all at once.

After an hour of this, Adam could not take it anymore. The tension kept his pulse quick, his senses heightened. The fear kept him wanting to go back to the safety of his tent. Even after this adventure the sound still made no sense to him. He headed back to his bed.

In the morning, he began asking questions again. He asked his fellow campers and he even asked his counselor, who abruptly said he knew nothing, and then changed the subject.

Over lunch, he and the other campers in his tent discussed the rumbling sound, and the counselor began to get agitated.

"You know this topic is not allowed at camp," he said to them, "so stop talking about it."

He was acting like it was dangerous to even talk

about it! Adam scoffed.

As if their *words* put them at risk or something! Adam was angry about the attitude that the camp and his counselor had. *It was childish to avoid talking about this*, he thought. They sat in silence for the rest of lunch, but Adam was not yet ready to give up on it. When the meal was over and everyone began heading back, Adam approached the boys from the most senior tent on boy's side.

"What do you know about the rumbling noise?" He asked them bluntly.

Several of them brushed him off. One dismissed the conversation with a wave of his hand and an 'it's nothing to worry about'. But another one of them, a tall boy with blonde hair, looked at him and asked:

"Why are you asking? What do *you* know about the rumbling noise?"

"I know it comes from the forest," said Adam earnestly. "I went in last night."

The senior boys went silent. The tall blonde one took him aside.

"What is your name?" He asked.

"Adam," Adam replied.

"I don't think you should go into the forest again. Especially not at night." said the boy, looking him seriously in the eye.

"Why?" Adam was very fast to respond. He felt he might finally get some answers from this guy.

"Because... Because there's a story about a boy who went in there once. It didn't turn out well." He said simply, trying to end the conversation.

"What do you mean? Did he... Not come back or something?"

"No," said the tall boy, raising his eye brows. "He came back. But he'd bitten off his own tongue to stop himself from screaming."

And with that, the tall boy turned away to join the other senior boys and Adam was left alone, his mind reeling. When night fell, Adam had made up his mind. Horror stories or no horror stories, he was going back into the forest. When all the others were asleep again, he dressed and headed out. He headed past the sign he'd seen the night before.

Keep the Silence.
Keep the Peace.

He followed the sound deeper and deeper into the forest until once again it was difficult to locate. Was it in front of him?

Behind him?

Sometimes it sounded like it was in more than one place. Sometimes it sounded like it was everywhere at once. He had the odd feeling that there was something in the trees around him. At one point the rumbling became so loud that he stopped where he was, his heart beating a hundred miles an hour, frightened whatever it was would jump out and take him.

In one striking moment he heard a new sound; the sound of someone or something breathing. He screamed.

He screamed and ran through the forest as fast as his legs would take him, the sound of rumbling suddenly blaring through the trees as if through a megaphone. As he bolted he tripped on an odd rock and stumbled.

His breath caught in his chest and he rolled into a bush. He lay still and silent with the rumbling, loud as a live rock concert, persisting through the trees.

He waited to see what was going to happen to him. He waited. He was still. He was silent.

After several moments, the rumbling faded. He got up and made his way quickly and quietly back to bed. When he got inside the tent, he changed into his pajamas. A voice out of the dark called softly to him.

"Adam," it said.

Adam jumped.

"Who's that?"

"It's me, Zach. What were you doing?"

"I... I went into the forest."

"Why?"

"To find the rumbling noise."

As Adam changed, he heard the rumbling still. If anything, it was getting louder.

"Did you find it?" Zach asked.

"No. But I got close. I think it's an animal."

"An animal can't make that sound!" came Zach's hushed voice.

Adam heard the rumbling grow even louder, and he became worried.

"I don't know what it is," he said. "But there might be more than one. Whatever it is, it's not normal."

"Do you think it's dangerous?"

Suddenly, with the rumbling noise louder than it had ever been in the tent, he thought he heard the sound of something move in the bushes nearby.

"Shhhh," whispered Adam desperately. "It can hear us."

The two boys fell silent.

Over the next sixty seconds, the sound slowly faded and the two boys went back to bed in silence.

The next day Adam's counselor pulled him aside and took him to the director's office.

The director sat him down and told him that someone had come forward.

He had been seen creeping out during the night.

The director had called Adam's parents.

He was going home.

Adam went back to his tent to pack his things. He felt angry. There was something happening that no one was being honest about. There was something in the forest, and no one was going to tell him what it was. Adam stopped packing his things.

He was going back into that forest, right now. He would wait until the sun went down, and he would find out what made the rumbling noise. Then, and only then, would he go home. So Adam ran from the tent and headed deep into the forest.

When Adam's parents arrived, no one could find him. They sent out a search party, but by then, the sun was setting. No one on the island was willing to search after the sun had set. Adam's parents were angry and confused. They needed to find their son. The idea that no one would search because it had gotten *dark* was preposterous to them. If no one was going to search for him, they would do it themselves.

The staff of camp advised them not to go. They said it was unsafe. They said the two of them should stay in and search in the morning. But they needed to find their boy. So, with the rumbling noise echoing across camp grounds, the two parents headed off down one of the forest trails.

By the time the sun rose the next day, the police were comforting Adam's parents at front reception whilst the search party restarted their searching.

Adam's parents had not slept. When the police asked them what happened, they said that around midnight they heard their son screaming and screaming.

By one o'clock the screaming had stopped, and they were still unable to find their boy anywhere. They had searched until the sun rose, when the search party was willing once again to continue scouring the island for their dear son. They had no more information about where he was, just the chilling memory of his desperate screams in the dead of the night, and the dark of the forest.

Adam's parents were absorbed in their despair as the police officer comforted them.

"There's a sign in the forest, did you know?" His father was saying as he held his sobbing wife.

"The last line is written in blood. It says:

Keep the silence.
Keep the peace.
Keep your life.

The Red Buoy

There is an old yellow canoe at the dock. It's many decades old, close to a century. Despite its age, the campers still take it out on camping trips. Its solid structure and craftsmanship make it a worthy vessel for such voyages into the unknown. The senior campers were preparing for their six-day adventure through the islands, and were glad to hear that they would be taking the old yellow canoe. It wouldn't be the same without it.

The senior campers set out. The days were long and the paddling dreary. They woke early in the mornings and paddled hard to get to their next camping site as the sun rose over their heads. They were only a few days into the trip when they saw that Red Buoy. Their canoe bobbed up and down on the waves as they passed it. It made no sense, really. The buoy sat alone on the body of water, and didn't seem to be marking or indicating anything at all. As they drifted by, one of the campers reached out to stroke it. Roughly splattered in dark paint was a droopy sad face along one side.

They all looked skyward as they passed.

A cloud moved in front of the sun, throwing their boat into a cold shadow. The canoe tilted to one side and then the other as waves developed unexpectedly around them. The weather was changing rapidly before their eyes. They clung to their seats as the water became rocky and uncomfortable, salty water splashing over into the boat. The wind gained force and lifted the hairs on their arms with an unnatural chill. With the waves now crashing heavily upon the boat, the canoe swayed dangerously from side to side and water poured in from all directions. The campers began to panic.

The storm gained momentum with every passing second and quite suddenly they were capsized. The campers surfaced and their counselor, Dan, desperately counted them. One, two, three. Four, five, six. They were safe. They managed to return the canoe to its proper position and they all clambered, soaking wet, into it.

They all gasped for breath, looking skyward once again. The sun shone overhead, warming their skin. It was like the weather had never changed. The counselor looked about. Most of their equipment was now either sinking to the sea floor, or floating away on the tide. They paddled about, collecting what they could.

The water was not only calmer than it was just minutes ago, but calmer than it had been in days. It was entirely flat and still, like glass. The only ripples in the water were the ones made with the movement of the boat as it stabilized.

It felt as though they were floating in a swimming pool or small lake, though the islands around them hung in view, far and distant.

The counselor made the call that they were to make their way to the closest shore. They needed a stock-take of what they had lost to see if their trip should finish early. The campers began to paddle, the nose of the boat pointed south toward land and toward safety.

With firm, strong strokes they moved powerfully through the still waters. The old yellow canoe lunged forward with every stroke, most easily in the stillness of the glassy water. It was after one hour of paddling, however, that the campers and their leader agreed that something was most certainly wrong.

Although they felt themselves moving forward, the shore did not come nearer. No matter how hard and fast they paddled, the shore remained distant and untouchable. After two hours of straight paddling, they took a break. With the sun beating down on them, and nothing to drink, they were exhausted and no nearer to their destination than when they began.

They sat in silence, and their boat became still on the water. Nothing moved. The water sat like glass beneath them. They all looked about at the strangeness of their situation. One of the campers gasped quite suddenly, and then began to cry. They all looked to her.

"What's wrong, Jenna?"

She pointed one shaky finger behind them. There, only a few short paddling strokes away, sat the red buoy, still and silent on the water. It was almost close enough to touch.

Two hours of paddling, and they had not moved even a foot.

They began to panic. It didn't make sense.

Dan dove into the water to find if any kind of line or chain had secured them to the buoy, or anything near it, but he found nothing. The old yellow canoe sat free standing atop the sea waters. These were the best paddling conditions since their trip began, but they were unable to go anywhere at all.

Dan pushed at the canoe from where he sat in the water, and it glided forward, but somehow, inexplicably, it gained no distance. He could visibly see the canoe carving the water, and yet it did not progress from that cursed Red Buoy. He climbed back in.

They all resolved, then and there as they stared at The Red Buoy, to push harder than ever before.

Their paddles entered the water, and at their leader's firm command, they worked. They paddled hard and fast, harder and more valiantly than ever before, but though they saw the water beneath them glide by, they did not move. Each in turn would look behind them as they paddled, and despite the forward momentum they felt, the buoy remained as still and close as ever, and the shore never came closer.

It was an hour later that Dan noticed that the sun itself had not moved. According to his estimation, it had been early afternoon, perhaps one pm, for three hours. Though Dan knew now that they were in danger, he kept calm for the sake of his campers. With his mobile phone now on the sea floor, he didn't know what to suggest, except to keep paddling.

And so they did.

Within another hour the campers were exhausted, hungry, thirsty and afraid. The sun sat still and unmoving in the sky. They sat in despair.

One of the campers stood up in the canoe.

"Look there!" He called, pointing out across the water.

A small speedboat sped through the water not too far from where they floated. They all got steadily to their feet and began waving their arms and paddles in the air, shouting as loudly as their voices would allow.

"HELP! HEEELLLP US!"

"WE'RE STUCK!"

"SAVE US!"

The boat sped by them, the skipper ignoring them entirely. Too fast the boat was gone, and the campers sat heavily back down.

"How could he do that?" One camper asked. "How could he ignore us like that?"

Another camper spoke up grimly. "Unless he couldn't see or hear us."

"But we were so close," said another, "there's no way."

The counselor said nothing, wondering if it was possible that they had become invisible to the outside world as they floated here in limbo. A camper named Liam stood up.

"That's it," said Liam. "There's more than one way to reach the shore."

"Sit down, Liam!" Commanded Dan, but Liam ignored him. He dove into the water, attempting to swim to shore.

They all called out to him, calling him back to the boat, but he heeded none of their calls.

Dan, standing tall at the rear, demanded in a booming voice that he return immediately. Call out as he may, Liam did not return. Dan refused to leave the other campers to retrieve him.

After five minutes, it became clear that Liam's attempt was futile. He'd gone no further than ten feet from the boat and gained no more.

The counselor guided the canoe forward, and it drifted alongside Liam, who climbed in. Dan looked back. The Red Buoy still sat just a few feet behind them, as close as ever before. With Liam now safely in the boat, Dan took off his shirt and warned the other campers to stay still inside the canoe. It was time for drastic action. He dove into the water. He dove as deep as he could, but the sea floor reached far below him. He surfaced and swam steadily over to the Red Buoy, the campers watching him as he went. He grasped the buoy and it took his weight. He bobbed up and down on the water's surface.

He took a deep breath and plunged into the water. He grabbed hold of the chain anchoring the buoy to the sea floor, and pulled himself deeper and deeper. He was running out of breath when the sea floor loomed in sight. It was littered in a vast array of debris; everything from destroyed boats to camping equipment, supplies and people's personal possessions.

The counselor let go of the chain and swam to the surface where he gasped for breath. The first thing he heard when the water cleared his ears was the sound of his campers screaming. The wind had picked up and the clouds had returned.

The water was no longer calm and still. The waves had returned and were rocking the boat back and forth.

Dan's mind scrambled. *Had touching the buoy triggered the storm?!*

Dan swam desperately back to the boat. When he clambered inside he called the campers to arms.

They picked up their paddles to stabilize the boat. After two minutes of fierce work, the weather began to clear. They had survived. The sun returned, and so did the stillness of the water. They were safe again.

The counselor commanded the campers to paddle at top speed. With each stroke they launched themselves forward toward the shore. They battled valiantly against an invisible current, and they felt, as they did before, the vessel carve through the water. However, when the counselor looked back to The Red Buoy it still had not moved.

The campers and their counselor cast down their paddles in despair, collapsed into the canoe and lay staring at the harsh sun as it beat down on them. The time passed slowly by as they lay in silence. Many of them gave up, believing they would die here in the middle of this desert of water.

Suddenly one of the campers yelled out, jumping to her feet.

"HEYYYYYYYYYYY!!!!" She called, waving her arms. The others looked up.

"HEEEEYYYYYYYYYYYYY!!!!!" She called again. It was a cargo ship, and it was heading directly toward them. They all leapt to their feet. With the sudden movement, the boat rocked and two campers tumbled into the water.

The rest yelled and cried out, waving their arms and drawing attention to their boat. The cargo ship cruised towards them at a great speed, and it seemed that their salvation might very well have arrived.

Dan watched the cargo ship and wondered about the change in weather just moments before - *Could this ship have broken through?*

As the cargo ship neared them it lost traction in the water and its speed dropped. It was odd, though, for by all the laws of physics it didn't appear to be slowing down. The sea sprayed up by the stern, the wake of the boat rippled behind it as if it were travelling at full speed, but the ship itself had slowed to a stop in front of them. Despite all appearances of high speed, it was no longer going anywhere.

A door opened on the deck, and an older bearded man stepped out.

"Hello down there!" He called.

The campers screamed out in joy in relief.

"Help us please! We're stuck here!"

"What're you doing out here so late at night? And – hey, blimey!" The man looked skyward. "The sun's come back out! Hey! Hey Barry!" The man moved back to the door. "Oi down there! I'll be right back! I just gotta get Barry to see this sun!"

The man disappeared into the ship, and the campers waited for him to return, grinning from ear to ear, overjoyed that they weren't alone, and that together there might finally be a way out of here.

The door opened and the bearded man stepped back onto the deck.

"Hello!" Dan called to the man.

"Hello down there!" called the bearded man.

"We're so glad you're here – we've been stranded for hours!"

"Can you call for help, we need the coast guard!" Called a camper.

"What're you doing out here so late at night? And – hey, blimey!" The man looked skyward again. "The sun's come back out! Hey! Hey Barry!"

Dan stared at him. He didn't know what to think. *What was wrong with this man?*

"Oi down there!" The bearded man called. "I'll be right back! I just gotta get Barry to see this sun!"

He disappeared again into the ship, and left them all on the water, confused and on the edge of hysterics.

"What happened?" asked one of the campers. "Doesn't he remember us?"

No one answered her, but waited in silence. After a moment, the door opened and again the man stepped out, calling down to them.

"Hello down there!" called the bearded man.

"No..." Whispered Dan to himself, his voice quavering.

"What're you doing out here so late at night? And — hey, blimey! The sun's come back out! Hey! Hey Barry!"

The campers and the counselor watched in a heavy silence as the man went through the entire performance for a third time. He discovered them, he discovered the sun, and disappeared once more into the ship to find Barry. He came out a fourth time, in the exact same way, and a fifth time.

He came out a sixth time.

A seventh time.

One of the campers began to cry.

The counselor didn't know what to do. As the minutes rolled by they all sat down and said nothing. The man continued to come out and call to them, but they ignored him.

"What're you doing out here so late at night? And — hey, blimey!"

After a moment, one of the campers spoke.

"It must be tomorrow everywhere else, except here."

The counselor nodded.

They all got to work finding anything they could

cover themselves up with so that they could block out the sun and get some sleep. They all drifted off at different times, and awoke at different times. The sun didn't move and none of them had a watch, so there was no way to tell what the time was or how long they'd been asleep.

When they were all awake some hours later, Dan had a plan to get some food. He dove into the water and swam over to the buoy. Ignoring the repetitive callings of the bearded man from the cargo ship, he dove down under the water.

Dan succeeding in pulling a small dry bag from the debris, and it floated to the surface. Drawing a deep breath, he examined the bag. It was labeled.

FOOD

Dan grasped the red buoy for balance before swimming slowly back to the canoe which sat still and unmoving on the glassy water. By the time he reached it, however, the water had one again become rocky and the waves threatened to throw them all into the water.

Working together, they kept the boat afloat until the waves had passed, the winds had died down and the clouds disappeared.

Whilst the campers tore apart the bag, pulling out pasta salad and tortillas, the counselor's mind was on something else.

"It's still good!" Said a camper. "Fresh as a daisy!"

"Nothing changes here," said another. "The food doesn't go bad."

"But it will run out," said Liam, with a mouth full of tortilla. Dan's mind was working fast, putting the pieces together.

"The sun's come back out! Hey! Hey Barry!" called the bearded man to no one.

Once the food had gone, the campers looked stronger than they had been in a long time. Dan got their attention.

"Listen up guys," he said. "We're going to do something now. And I want you to follow my instructions very closely. This is very important. Do *everything* I tell you, understood?"

They nodded.

The counselor dived once again into the water; fresh and cool after the harshness of the sun. He swam steadily out to the buoy. Once he reached it, he hesitated. He called back to his campers.

"Is everyone ready?"

"Yesss..." They all called back.

He gripped the red buoy with his hands, and he could see that creepy sad face in dark drippy paint half submerged in the water. He abandoned the buoy and swam at full speed back to the boat.

The clouds gathered above them and the wind picked up.

The waves were tumultuous and he was barely able to get into the boat.

"ALRIGHT," he called out to his campers over the sound of the wind. "EVERYONE FLIP THE BOAT!"

They all screamed out in protest.

"DO IT NOW!" He screamed, and they followed his instruction.

The entire boat flipped, capsized, and they were all thrown under the water. The silence pressed in on all their ears.

When they surfaced, they splashed about in the waves, gasping breaths of air. Dan screamed out to them to climb into the boat and paddle as fast as they could. They climbed in, scrabbling about for oars as they went.

The sound of the bearded man screaming met their ears as they began to paddle. The waves crashed heavily into his cargo ship. It was an incredible thing to see, the waves taking the massive metal structure in its grasp and tossing it carelessly about. All the campers screamed as they saw the bearded man topple into the water and the entire cargo ship tilted deeply to one side. It was so far over that water rushed up on the deck. It continued to flip, and the campers saw the keel of the massive thing emerge from the water and point toward the sky.

The cargo ship had capsized. What happened next was even stranger. The campers watched in horror as the bearded man splashed about next to his capsized cargo ship.

His voice began to fade from their ears, and quite oddly, the ship, the man and everything about them began to vanish into thin air, leaving nothing behind them but open water.

The clouds cleared, the sun came out. The wind died down and the waves slowed to a basic steady rocking. The all pushed steadily forward in their canoe. Dan looked behind them.

The Red Buoy had disappeared.

After fifteen minutes of paddling they could see the rocks and trees get closer with every stroke. The last thing they heard as they made their way towards the shore was the voice of the bearded man echoing across the water as if from nowhere.

"Hey Barry!" It said. "Barry, this might sound crazy, but I don't think we're actually movin'! It looks like we are, but the shore... It just dudn't get 'nee nearer, Barry..."

The Clay Army
Original Concept by Thomas Lind

Nicole couldn't shake the funny feeling she got around camp. There was something militant about it, something army-like, something unusually *prepared*, there really was. Maybe it was just the strange dreams she had, vivid dreams, of a hundred uniformed men marching in time, of the call of a lieutenant and the soldiers' chanting response. It certainly wasn't anything anyone said or did. Camp was such a wonderful, carefree place. Nicole had been coming here since she was old enough to come. Like her mother before her, and her grandmother before that.

Nicole tried to shake the feeling. She spent her summer days at the barn, riding the days away along the beaches or forest trails, or in the paddock working on her canter. It was a beautiful thing to see the sunset from the back of a horse, without a care in the world.

Nicole and the other campers had only been at camp a few days when it all began.

In the mornings campers woke to find their possessions displaced or missing.

This was enough to cause arguments. Each camper had their suspicions. Every camper had someone in their tent that they didn't like, and had convinced themselves that this was the person to blame.

If it is a single camper doing all of this, thought Nicole to herself, *he or she must be working very hard.*

Then there was something else, too. Nicole noticed the cuts and scratches on her arms and legs but told no one about them. It was the other campers that spoke up in confusion. They went to bed fresh and clean, and when the sun rose, some of them would be sporting curious wounds and injuries that no one was able to explain. Only small things they were; no severed limbs, no missing toes. It was small enough for the counselors to brush off and say —

"You must have done that yesterday during capture the flag."

Nicole knew that this wasn't the first time this had happened at camp. She remembered similar events last year, and the year before, and even before that. It didn't make sense, and the campers knew it. Rumors began to fly; incredible stories of fiction spread to explain the strangeness of these occurrences. Everything from bed bugs to vampires that lived in the woods, from voodoo dolls to bad camp food reacting with their skin. A small group of younger boys were convinced that gnomes came into their tents at night to take their things and punish them for behaving badly at camp.

"Psst," came a hushed whisper.

It was morning; they had just finished breakfast, and Nicole was on her way back to her cabin alone. She stopped.

"Psst, Nicole!" came the call again.

She looked around. It was her friend Lilly. Lilly was frantically gesturing for her to follow. Nicole stepped from the path into the overgrowth.

"Lilly, what are you-"

"Nicole," she breathed, excited. "Half past eleven, meet me at the old apple tree by the garden. *Don't be late.*"

"Lilly, I can't, I have inkle-weaving-"

"Not half past eleven this morning," she said, disappearing into the trees with a sly grin. "Half past eleven tonight."

Nicole couldn't believe she was doing this. It was dark, it was cold, and she could get in so much trouble for this. She'd probably be kicked out of camp. She almost changed her mind. She waited by the old apple tree as her watch ticked over to half past eleven. She shivered.

"Thanks for coming."

Nicole turned around. Lilly was leaning against the wooden fence panels.

"Are you ready for this?"

"Why are we here, Lilly? This is stupid."

Lilly ignored her and took her by the arm.

"But – where are we going-?"

Half an hour later Nicole still had no answers. They were standing by the paddock, whispering to one another, when Lilly hushed her.

"Shhhhh," she said. She watched her watch as it clicked over to twelve O'clock. "It's midnight."

Nicole was getting annoyed now. Every time she tried to speak Lilly shushed her. Nicole's frustration dissolved to instant fear as something quivered in the dark in front of her.

There was something moving in the trees. In fact, it

wasn't *something*, it was *a lot of things*.

People stumbled forth from the trees, walking slowly, faces blank and eyes closed. Ten, twenty, fifty, a hundred; more and more emerged, stumbling into the moonlight. Nicole stifled a scream. She couldn't believe what she was seeing. She fought the desire to run. If this was the zombie apocalypse, they should head for the mainland immediately.

Nicole blinked. The slow, stumbling figures were all wearing pajamas.

"Hey," she said, "that's Jenna! HEY, JENNA!"

Lilly covered Nicole's mouth and hissed in her ear.

"Shhhhhh, they're asleep!"

Nicole fell silent in shock. "Are — are they dangerous?"

Nicole watched as all her fellow campers and counselors made their way across the field in their own time. Even the camp director was there, his face blank, his eyes closed, wearing boxer shorts and a tank top.

"No," answered Lilly. "They're just doing their duty."

Nicole gaped at her.

"C'mon," giggled Lilly. "Let's see where they go."

It was a scary thing to see, all those people making their way in the night, silent but somehow organized. As they headed into the forest they bumped into trees and tripped over branches.

They always picked themselves up and continued blindly forward. Eventually, they reached an open clearing in the forest, where they gathered in perfect lines all facing forward. They stood silent and still for two minutes as Lilly and Nicole watched. Quite suddenly, they chanted.

"SIR, YES SIR."

The group of them, aged from just eight years to late fifties began to march in perfect co-ordination, as if they had been training for years. It was mesmerizing to watch, and Nicole couldn't believe it.

"Hang on," said Nicole as she began to catch on. She looked at her arms and legs. "*Lilly, was I here last night?!*"

Lilly looked sympathetically at her.

"Come with me," she murmured quietly.

The two of them left the rest of camp population behind, but the sound of the marching and chanting followed them as they made their way between the trees. After ten minutes the two of them began to hear other voices ahead. Out of the darkness loomed a small group of people.

"Speak of the devil. Nicole, it's good of you to join us."

"James?"

Nicole was in shock. There were five people standing before her, James from pottery class being one of them. Behind those five, there seemed to be a personal guard of three sleeping senior campers. Their arms were held tightly by their sides, their backs straight as they awaited instruction.

Nicole couldn't believe it.

"What is this, precisely?" She spoke up into the dark silence. "Anyone care to explain all this to me?"

"Well, where to begin..." James looked at the other members of the group.

"What is that?" asked Nicole, suddenly noticing a collection of clay figurines sitting on top of a tree stump.

"Oh, that's us." answered James simply. Nicole took a closer look.

He was right, there were seven of them standing around, including Nicole, and there were seven simple clay figures. Each was no more than a clay pillar with a head on top of it, except the heads looked kind of like comical versions of the real campers. Nicole could pick out which one was her. Her head was on sideways.

"Who made these?"

"We did," said a tall boy Nicole didn't know. "It's the only way to escape the sleepwalking army. You must place a clay figure here to replace you. It's been going on for years."

Nicole listened to the sounds of the chanting still echoing behind her. She couldn't believe she had unknowingly been a part of it the whole time.

"You... Released me?" she asked. "Why?"

"We needed someone to replace Justin."

"What happened to Justin?"

They hesitated. A girl Nicole knew from horseback riding spoke up.

"Camp Kiljoi. They destroyed the clay version of him. We only just got back in time to save the rest."

Nicole gaped at a girl named Pamela, who went on.

"They have an army like ours. Each camp sends our armies over to destroy the clay figurines of the other camp. They destroyed Justin's figure, and he went back to sleep and re-joined the army."

"You can't just... Make another figurine of him?"

They all shook their head.

"Once it's destroyed, the person can't come back. They forget everything they've learned and have no idea any of this is happening.

People can only be released once, and it only works if you place their clay figure here, on this tree stump."

Nicole stared at the stump.

"Why are we fighting camp Kiljoi?" Nicole asked slowly.

"They started it," said the tall boy.

They ignored him. Pamela spoke.

"If we succeed in destroying their clay figures, there's no one left to lead their army. It's the only way to completely defend our camp." She explained.

"Who leads our army?"

"We do," answered Lilly. "They do as we command, as the only free thinkers of camp."

This was a lot for Nicole to swallow. Nicole wouldn't have believed a word if she had not just seen the army with her own eyes.

"Anyway!" Lilly clapped her hands together. "Talking about commands, should we go and give orders?"

Nicole followed along as the group went back to the army. Standing before them, they gave orders. Some were to guard The Clay Army, others were to form an operative and sneak into Camp Kiljoi.

Over the next two hours, Nicole watched in awe as the battle was waged. The first time Nicole saw the campers of Camp Kiljoi swarming onto camp property, she was directly in their path. She screamed, frozen in fear. The sleepwalking kitchen chef barreled in to save her, tackling an eight year old boy dressed in Family Guy pajamas.

The night was a failure on both sides, and this seemed usual. Nicole was exhausted and glad to finally head back to bed.

As she crept under her covers in her cabin, so did her fellow campers. In dead silence, her sleep-walking friends lay down to sleep. After two minutes, it was like they'd never left.

When they awoke in the morning, Nicole was tired, but the other campers were not. They were merely confused as to how Meryl has obtained a large bruise on her leg.

Over the coming week, Nicole, Lilly and the others launched numerous attacks on camp Kiljoi, whilst securing their own borders. It was a dangerous but noble fight. There were people running all over both camps, dead asleep but full of energy.

"Doesn't anyone ever get killed?" asked Nicole one night, concerned.

"*Of course not,*" said Lilly, shocked. "We're not *murderers!*"

It was true. It seemed very defensive, each camp trying to protect its own. Nicole became quite adept at giving orders, and loved to give the most dangerous tasks to Meryl, whom she did not like very much.

One night, Lilly found Nicole by Lake Ann whilst the battle was fought in the trees all around her.

She was just staring at the lake, lost in thought.

"What *are* you doing?" Lilly, giggled.

Nicole looked around.

"Oh, nothing," she said.

Lilly stood by the lake with Nicole.

"There are a lot of stories about this lake," said Lilly.

"I know," Nicole was very thoughtful. After a moment, Nicole spoke up. "My grandmother used to tell me that there's gold at the bottom, but it's guarded by monsters."

"C'mon," said Lilly. "Let's get back to the fight."

To Lilly, Nicole seemed distracted, but she soon settled back into throwing orders to her fellow snoring campers, and before they knew it, the battle was over — another fruitless night for both teams.

Both clay armies remained intact in their respective camps.

Nicole continued her horse riding by day, and her battling of sleepy armies by night. It was a lifestyle she could never have imagined.

It was a week or two later, and they were all hard at work. Most of the free-thinking crew had assembled by the camp border, and were discussing tactics.

"Camp Kiljoi were coming from the South last night, they could be doing it again as a diversion tonight." Pamela was saying, but stopped very suddenly when she looked at James.

"James, are you okay?" She asked quickly. James looked very sleepy. In fact, he couldn't keep his eyes open.

"Oh, no," said Lilly, terror tearing through her body. James collapsed, asleep, on the ground as the tall boy began to yawn.

He couldn't hold it back, despite the look of sheer terror on his face.

"Camp Kiljoi," said Lilly, "THEY'VE BROKEN THROUGH!"

The lot of them raced back between the trees to get to the tree stump, wondering how its sleeping guard had been defeated. They were dropping like flies. They were twenty seconds from the figures, and all but Pamela and Lilly had succumbed to sleep and fallen behind. Lilly looked behind her in horror as Pamela yawned and fell behind.

The tree stump came into view, and there was only one person standing over it, hammer in hand, shattered clay lying all over the forest floor.

Lilly was too late.

She arrived just in time to see the heavy mallet fall upon her own clay figurine, which exploded upon impact. She fell to her knees in front of the tree stump as her whole body began to ache with tiredness.

"Why?" She asked, looking up at the perpetrator she had so willingly brought into their circle of trust. It was Nicole.

"I'm sorry Lilly," she said, "I have something I need to do."

And with a last longing look at her friend, Lilly closed her eyes and drifted off to sleep. Nicole stood over her. After a moment, the sleeping Lilly got up from the forest floor and made her way blindly through the trees, bumping and tripping as she went.

Nicole followed her. The battle was soon over, and she called the army to assemble in the forest clearing.

As the lone free-thinker of camp, she was now entirely in control.

"ATTEN-TION!"

Straight-backed and silent, the army looked to Nicole.

"Okay everybody," she began. "There's something at the bottom of Lake Ann, and you're going to help me get it."

Epilogue

Nicole could hear the sound of rasping, screeching and moaning swamp monsters battling a hundred sleep-walking campers as she stood alone in the forest. Empty cans of shaving cream littered the woods from one side of camp to the other. One of the senior boys appeared by her side, eyes closed and blank-faced. He awaited orders. Nicole grinned slyly.

"Thomas," began Nicole. "I hear you have a counselor who likes to tell stories."

Thomas remained still and silent.

"I think you should suggest some to him."

Nicole giggled to herself.

Why not? She thought.

They'll never believe them anyway.

Goodnight, Royal.

41671387R00065

Made in the USA
Charleston, SC
05 May 2015